BRAVE
IN THE
WOODS

Also by Tracy Holczer

The Secret Hum of a Daisy
Everything Else in the Universe

BRAVE
IN THE
WOODS

TRACY HOLCZER

putnam

G. P. PUTNAM'S SONS

G. P. PUTNAM'S SONS

An imprint of Penguin Random House LLC, New York

Visit us online at penguinrandomhouse.com

Library of Congress Cataloging-in-Publication Data
Names: Holczer, Tracy, author.
Title: Brave in the woods / Tracy Holczer.
Description: New York: G. P. Putnam's Sons, [2021] | Summary: "After her
brother goes missing in Afghanistan, twelve-year-old Juni sets out to break a family
curse in hopes it will bring her brother safely home"—Provided by publisher.
Identifiers: LCCN 2020040774 (print) | LCCN 2020040775 (ebook) |
ISBN 9781984813992 (hardcover) | ISBN 9781984814005 (ebook)
Subjects: CYAC: Missing persons—Fiction. | Grief—Fiction. |
Brothers and sisters—Fiction. | Blessing and cursing—Fiction.
Classification: LCC PZ7.H6974 Br 2021 (print) | LCC PZ7.H6974 (ebook) |
DDC [Fic]—dc23
LC record available at https://lccn.loc.gov/2020040774
LC ebook record available at https://lccn.loc.gov/2020040775

Printed in the United States of America
ISBN 9781984813992
1   3   5   7   9   10   8   6   4   2

Design by Suki Boynton
Text set in Janson MT Pro

For Kevin,
my partner in the woods
and in the light.

No one knows the strength of
kindred love until it is tried.

ELIZABETH KEEGAN, 12 years old, 1852

VELVET BONES

JUNIPER FELT IT when her brother disappeared.

She was certain of this.

Oddly, her lungs didn't go all wonky the way they sometimes did when bad things happened. Like a hive of bees was inside her chest, using up every bit of her breath with their buzzing and swarming.

That feeling would come later.

Instead, when she startled awake at 2:37 in the morning on July 6—eleven and a half hours behind Afghanistan time and the explosion that started everything—she had the astonishing feeling of antlers growing in. So much so that she jumped out of bed and switched on the twinkle lights above her mirror to make sure she wasn't turning into a woodland creature out of a fairy tale.

And there, clear as her startled expression, she saw them. The fierce velvet antlers of a blacktail deer.

Then they were gone, leaving Juni to hope she'd been dreaming, or she'd lost her marbles, or both. Either would have been better than the third possibility.

Juni climbed back into bed—alongside Penelope the foster cat—and told herself it was her imagination. Because of course it was. Her grandmother Anya had been reading to Juni, Connor and their father before them the fairy tales of the Brothers Grimm for as long as she could remember. Anya wanted them to understand the truth in the fairy tales, as gruesome as they were, so they might be prepared for life's twists and turns. Honest stories, Anya had reasoned, helped people make sense of the world as it really was instead of the way everyone wished it would be.

But Juni believed Anya's motivation went deeper than that, even if she would never admit it properly. Because if their family legend was to be believed, they were cursed.

Dad didn't believe in the Grimm family legend, that the descendants of Jacob and Wilhelm Grimm were cursed to endure the worst of the treacherous fairy tales, penance for crossing a witch once upon a time. He liked to point out how no one in their family had ever fallen asleep for a thousand years or married a king or eaten a poisoned apple or been turned into a frog. And while that was all technically accurate, Juni had often wondered if it was the spirit of the fairy tales that haunted them more than the literal tales themselves. Their family was, after all, prone to extreme luck, both good and bad.

No one knew this better than Juni, who was certain she had used up whatever good luck she'd been allotted simply by being born. Three miracles was what it had taken to save her. She'd cheated Death, and everyone knew Death was a sore loser.

Juni looked up at the mural on her wall. Specifically, the watercolor Connor had painted of a ten-point buck just before he left for basic training all those months ago. It was meant to be a reminder that she had survived. The buck had been a witness.

This calmed her. Between the buck being the last thing she saw before going to sleep each night, and a lifetime of stories about a family curse, it was no wonder Juni had dreamed a fairy-tale sort of dream. So, with nothing to be done in the middle of the night, she forced the whole shebang straight out of her mind and let Penelope's soft purr lull her back to sleep. Morning was the only antidote to crazy midnight imaginings. All she had to do was get there.

But the antler dream haunted her. And when they found out Connor had gone missing in action later that very day, Juni couldn't stop thinking about the curse, how the two might be connected. There was no antidote for that. Except one only Anya could provide.

Juni tried to be logical. She didn't want to burden Anya with her crazy antler problem when they were all going through so much. But finally, three agonizing days later, with the feeling she was about to come apart at the joints and fall into a pile of bones, Juni couldn't help herself.

They sat in matching Adirondack chairs on the deck, quietly watching a summer storm build over the water. Before the valley was flooded to become Lake Almanor, the Great Western Power Company had moved a Maidu reservation and cemetery, and Anya had always said that when thunder rolled in the sky, and whitecaps rose on the water, it was the justifiable rage of the Maidu.

There were still forests of pine trees on the bottom, and four-foot-long catfish swimming among the branches. The lake was a melancholy place that Juni felt matched the deepest part of herself.

"Deer are often the symbol of an impending journey," Anya said. "Sometimes your sleeping mind knows what your wakeful mind does not."

"I don't think I was sleeping when I saw the antlers."

"Does it matter?"

"Sure. Dreaming is normal. Seeing things is crazy."

"Normal? Crazy? We see what we see."

Thunder rumbled. The sky turned dark and threatening. Penelope jumped into Juni's lap and tucked her paws under her own soft body. Gray like a shadow, Penelope matched the storm clouds and Juni's mood.

Juni whispered, "But what if he's gone missing because of the curse? What if the dream is trying to tell me something?"

"Oh, Juni girl, look at me." Anya took Juni's chin in her palm. There were smudges under Anya's eyes. None of them had slept. "I had no business putting those ideas in your head. They were the silly ramblings of your superstitious old grandmother trying to make sense of her own life. Can you understand that?"

But Anya looked scared, which scared Juni.

The curse had always been feathery to Juni, like a cirrus cloud, because Anya had never really explained its origin. Nor did she talk much about her own childhood story. Instead, Juni and Connor had followed Anya around in the garden and the woods, along the creeks and rivers and on the lake, as she wove stories of distant family with the fairy tales of the Brothers Grimm until all that darkness and wonder had blended into an irresistible stew. It coursed through Juni's veins and wrapped around her heart and had her believing that her own miraculous survival, and her life yet to be lived, was part of some vast fairy tale she didn't yet understand.

"But look what happened to you, to Grandpa Charlie and now to Connor. The stories you've told about the rest of the family . . ."

"Enough, Juni! We are in charge of our own stories, not the other way around." Anya's hand fluttered to her mouth. "No more talk of curses. Promise me."

"Okay, Anya. I promise."

Juni was left even more shaken. She'd never seen Anya in such a state.

Over the days that followed, Juni desperately tried to talk herself out of believing the curse was real, that there was any meaning in her vision of antlers. It was as Anya had said—her sleeping brain had given her a symbol. That was all. She tried to believe she was no more cursed to grow deer antlers than she was to find herself trapped inside the body of a fox.

But she couldn't. No matter how hard Juni tried, she just couldn't shake the feeling of those new velvet bones taking hold. That alongside losing something precious, she had gained something impossible.

FRECKLE GROWING

FLAT ON THE sunporch floor, propped on her elbows, Juni stared through the screen as the rising August sun lit the pine trees, a glass of lemonade with a bendy straw tilted into her mouth.

Where is he where is he where is he?

In the thirty-two days since they'd found out Connor had gone missing, the worry had never left Juni's mind.

Not when she tried to read *The One and Only Ivan* for the seventh time because it was her favorite book ever. Not when she worked with Anya all day turning blackberries into jam. Not when she climbed the magical juniper tree, for which she was named, to sit in the old saddle Connor had loosely tied to the widest branch.

Especially not then.

She worried about being cursed. She worried about the bees in her chest. She worried that school was about to happen to her again. How was she supposed to get up every morning and think about math and English and social studies when her brother had vanished? How was she supposed to sit at a school desk five miles away when the army man could come back at any moment and tell her family they'd found Connor?

If her brain was a pie, nine-tenths of it would be Connor is Missing in Afghanistan and one-tenth would be Everything Else. Like the thought of eighth-grade PE next year with Mr. Snickleman—who, when he learned she had the nonallergic type of asthma and wasn't allowed to run, informed her it was a mental condition—which made her want to burrow into the deepest part of her closet and never come out.

"Juniper Creedy," Mom said from the kitchen. A long-drawn-out whisper-snap.

Juni jumped up, startled, knocking over her glass of lemonade. "Crap."

"I heard that," Mom said. Crap but her hearing was good.

Juni let herself through the screen door into the kitchen, where Mom had found her lemonade mess—the sugar she'd spilled on the counter alongside the lemons she'd squeezed, sticky juice already congealing. Juni hadn't gotten around to cleaning yet. She'd wanted to watch the trees catch the sunrise.

"I didn't think you'd be up," Juni said, reaching for a sponge.

"I've got it," Mom snapped again, level-ten exasperated already, and it wasn't even seven in the morning.

Mom's springy dark hair stuck out every which way and looked to Juni like a bunch of tiny antlers. She'd been seeing them everywhere now—in the branches of an aspen or the shadows crisscrossing the forest floor. She'd seen them in the clouds above the lake, and the formation of stones in the creek bed.

The only way Juni had found to get those antlers out of her head was to draw them on paper. So, she fetched her charcoals and sketchbook and slid into a wooden chair at the kitchen table. Juni also wanted to capture some piece of Mom with her charcoals before Mom dragged herself back to bed to watch *Gunsmoke* and *The Andy Griffith Show* all day on TV Land.

Mom was under the spell of the curse. Dad, too.

And Juni had proof: Mom and Dad thought Connor was gone. Not missing, but flat-out gone. There was nothing Juni could do to convince them otherwise. Even the army man had said, "Missing in action," but Mom and

Dad were determined to believe the worst, and believing the worst had stolen them away.

In the Grimm tales, loved ones were sometimes turned into animals when they'd been cursed, and Juni had begun to see her mother as a sleeping bird, nestled in her cage day after day, while Dad had turned into a bear roaming the woods, ferocious and growling and knocking things down.

Juni knew she had to find a way to bring them back, to bring Connor back, even if she had no idea where to begin. She'd been poring over her book of fairy tales, looking for clues, but hadn't found the answer yet.

As though hearing the call of Juni's worried heart, Penelope came trotting into the kitchen and jumped onto the table to lick her paw. She had yellow eyes, like little round lanterns. Juni took a short break from her sketch to scratch behind Penelope's ears, which made them both feel better.

It was a terrible time to bring it up, but Mom was out of her birdcage, which hadn't happened much in almost five weeks. "Did you hear yet? About Elsie?"

Mom was still scrubbing the sticky counter. She didn't turn around. "You have to stop pestering me about that dog. As soon as I know, you'll know."

"You said we might hear in a couple of weeks."

"It's been a couple of weeks?" Mom still didn't turn around. She was looking out the window toward the pasture and Cowabunga, their Jersey cow. "Have you seen Dad this morning?"

"He must have left before I woke up," Juni said, smudging the charcoal with her thumb. She'd managed one perfect ghostly antler growing from the curls on Mom's head. "Can I write the army another letter? Are you calling them every day?"

"I'm doing the best I can, Juniper."

Which wasn't true. Uncursed Mom would have been making seventeen phone calls a day. Because Elsie was Connor's military service dog, and in his first letter from Afghanistan he'd told them they had another member of the family in Elsie, the golden retriever he'd been assigned. Now that the army had retired Elsie after she'd been injured in the explosion, Juni expected she'd arrive at any moment. She belonged with them until Connor got home.

Because of course she did.

The cuckoo clock above the kitchen door cuckooed seven times. Mom finally turned from her cleaning and watched the little cuckoo Grandpa Charlie had carved, popping out again and again, like she'd had no idea what time it was until that very moment.

"I've asked you to stop getting up so early, Juni. You know your breathing gets funny when you're over-tired." But Juni knew it wasn't the getting-up-early part that bothered Mom. It was where Juni went at 6:20 every morning that Mom didn't like, even if she'd never stop her.

Mom reached for Juni's asthma pack on the kitchen counter. It didn't matter to her that premature babies often developed asthma and just as often grew out of it. What mattered to Mom was that Juni almost died when she was born. So now, and for as long as Juni could remember, she'd had to blow into a peak flow meter three times every day as well as make notes about her coloring and moisture levels. Because everyone wants a record of how sweaty and red-faced they get.

You're fragile, Juni. Try to remember that.

Mom's words were forever echoing in her head.

Just then, Anya shuffled into the kitchen, her white-gray pixie cut smoothed behind her ears, cat-eye glasses on a crystal chain around her neck. The remaining four foster cats came trotting in from the many nooks and crannies they'd hidden themselves in, Penelope joining them. She would be going to her permanent home in the next couple of days, and Juni was unbearably sad to see her go.

"What are you two arguing about now?" Anya said as she scooped wet food onto mismatched china dishes. The cats flicked their tails and chattered their complaints, letting her know she was late. "And where is that son of mine?"

"I'm being inconsiderate. Again," Juni said. "Sorry, Mom. I'll clean my mess sooner next time. And Dad's already gone for his walk."

Mom didn't answer, and the way the light hit her curls brought back a flash of memory. It had been a summer morning, just like this one, Mom beside her at the breakfast table, giggling. Mom was "giving her freckles," which consisted of pinching a freckle off her own arm, and then touching Juni's arm with it. When Mom would pull her finger away, magically, a freckle Juni would swear she'd never seen before sat underneath. Juni had been little enough to believe that all the freckles she owned came from her mother's freckle-giving powers, and she'd fling herself out of her chair and go shrieking through the house, "MOM GREW ME ANOTHER FRECKLE!"

Juni couldn't remember when she'd left that little piece of believing behind.

As Mom left the kitchen to go back upstairs, the phone rang. It was Mason Wheeler, one of Juni's best friends, who lived next door.

"Hey. I was just talking to Gabby and she's really hoping you'll be here tomorrow," he said.

Juni sighed. "Of course I'll be there."

Gabby's beloved rat, Piper, had died, and they were having a funeral at the ever-expanding Wheeler Family Pet Cemetery. Juni had already missed barbecues at the lake, the Paul Bunyan Festival and the Singin' with the Oldies musical marathon at the Mt. Lassen Theatre. She couldn't miss this, too, especially since she was about to miss something even more important.

Juni hadn't told Mason or Gabby yet, but she wasn't going on their annual just-before-school-starts camping trip to Domingo Springs even though it meant everything to all of them. Especially now.

"Why didn't she call me herself?"

"She didn't want to be a pain."

"But it's okay for you to be a pain?" Juni said. She was only half joking. It was like neither of them knew how to talk to her anymore.

"Well, we all know you could never be mad at me, so . . ."

"I'll call her," Juni said.

"What's going on?" Mason said. "I mean, besides the obvious."

"Nothing. I'm just tired."

"You know Gabby understands, right?"

But Juni wasn't so sure. Gabriella Carolina Tavares had a personal motto, "Grab Life by the Horns." She played club soccer like a gladiator and was the only kid Juni knew in middle school who kept an Anthology of Accomplishments that took up seven notebooks on half a bookshelf and went back to first grade. Gabby liked to repeat one of her father's favorite sayings: Si vale la pena hacerlo, vale la pena hacerlo bien. Anything worth doing is worth doing well. Gabby's father was a life coach, and Mr. Tavares was Gabby's hero.

Although Gabby would never come out and say, "Juniper! You have to live your life!" Juni couldn't help but feel that was exactly what Gabby was thinking.

"I'll be there," Juni said.

When she hung up, Juni took her charcoal drawing of Mom's curl-antlers and taped it to the kitchen wall with all the others. She stepped back and studied. There were now thirty-two antler drawings, one for every day since Connor went missing. Some large, some the size of a postage stamp. Napkins, receipts, notebook paper. Whatever was within reach. She had no idea what they might have to do with the curse, but she felt they were connected somehow.

Mom thought they were disturbing, and Dad didn't say what he thought, but Juni could see it right there on his face. The worry. Like maybe her compulsion to draw antlers was somehow his fault.

Anya came up behind Juni, looking over the collection. It was because of Anya that they were still on the wall. *My house, my taste in art* was what she'd told Mom and Dad. She seemed to understand they were necessary for Juni, even if she wouldn't let Juni talk about why.

"Did I ever tell you I gathered every manageable possession I had left of my family and wore them all tucked into the many pockets of a big raincoat Great-Grandpa Teddy gave me?"

Surprised by Anya's openness about her past, Juni shook her head. "You didn't."

Anya smoothed Juni's hair. "There is no right way to cope with a terrible situation. Whatever works is what you do."

Anya didn't talk much about the family she was born to other than the basic facts. That her parents had died, one right after the other, when she was eleven years old. How she and her brother, Will, had slipped through the cracks of social services for a time, living together in an old fishing shack their father had used in the woods near their home in South Lake Tahoe. When they were found, Will was sick, and he eventually died from pneumonia before Anya was sent to live in Chester with foster parents who eventually adopted her. Great-Grandpa Teddy and Great-Grandmother Abigail had brought Anya to this very house, and were loving and kind. But Anya had run away from them once, and never talked about why.

Anya touched the edge of Juni's latest antler drawing. "No good has ever come from believing in curses. Or fairy tales," she said.

Juni held her breath, hoping Anya would say more. Needing her to. But more wasn't coming.

She knew this was hard on Anya. Because of course it was. Anya was doing everything: cooking, cleaning and running their lives as best she could, filling in the gaps Connor's disappearance had left behind. Now it seemed she was forced to think extra hard about the family she'd lost so long ago. It must have been unbearable.

But how could she ask Juni not to believe something Juni believed?

"I'm scared," Juni whispered.

"It's hard not to be afraid when you don't have answers," Anya said.

She ran her hands over Juni's shoulders and squeezed,

like the quick wringing out of a sponge. "When I can't shake the fear, I go to the woods. I let those trees soak up the burden of it. They know what to do."

But Juni was certain there weren't enough woods or antler sketches or anything else big enough to soak up her terrible fears. That she'd stop breathing. That they were cursed.

That Connor would never be found.

CHEEZ WHIZ AND AARDVARKS

THE WHEELER FAMILY Pet Cemetery was created in 1946 by Mason's great-grandmother on his father's side, Anita Wheeler. Mrs. Wheeler loved her dog, Izzy, with every bit of her heart, and when the German shepherd leapt into the nearby Feather River—to save her only son, Mason Jr.—and died for her trouble, Mrs. Wheeler decided Izzy deserved a proper burial with a headstone, minister, one-gun salute from her sharpshooter friend, Bob, and every one of Izzy's dog friends from the neighborhood in attendance.

It was a miracle, after all. Or a fairy tale. Who could know at this point?

Because Izzy hadn't been at the river with Mason Jr. that day. She'd been sleeping on the porch at Anita

Wheeler's feet when she suddenly leapt up for no good reason, ran for all she was worth to the Feather River a quarter mile away and jumped in to save Mason Jr. just in the nick of time.

Later, as Izzy's dog friends began to die of old age, the owners asked if they could bury their beloved pets alongside her, and a pet cemetery sort of happened. And since he was alive instead of drowned in the Feather River, Mason Jr. went on to make the kinds of aerosol cans used for shaving cream and stuff, and made a fortune, which he then spent on several charity causes, one being a Save the African Mammals campaign. The story goes that Mrs. Wheeler went to her grave proud that by saving her son, Izzy was partly responsible for keeping the world in Cheez Whiz and aardvarks.

Even more important, though, Mason Jr. had been Anya's very best friend right up until he passed away ten years ago.

Anya didn't talk about that, either.

Mason loved his family story even though most people in their small Northern California town of Chester, population 2,144, thought he and his family were odd. They walked wide circles around Anya, too. Fairy-tale curses? Miraculous dogs? A pet cemetery? It didn't matter that Mr. Wheeler was the town veterinarian, or that Mrs. Wheeler was a sculptor with art in an actual San Francisco gallery, just like it didn't matter that Anya wrote cozy mysteries, a perfectly normal job. But it seemed their peculiarities were too much for the everyday cattle ranchers and timber millers in their everyday town.

This was one of the thousands of ways Juni and Mason were connected; he had his miraculous dog story and she had her Grimm family legend. The most important connection, though, was that Mason Harold Wheeler IV was the love of Juni's life, even if they hadn't kissed yet.

He'd tried once. There was a Sadie Hawkins dance at the end of seventh grade last year, and when Mr. Finster pretended to marry them, Mason, completely out of character, turned to kiss her. And since Juni had nowhere to go, she fell straight back into the haystacks. They had a discussion about being in agreement afterward, and Mason felt awful. He hadn't seen it as a "real" kiss, whatever that meant.

He should have felt bad. Not only because he didn't ask first, but because a first kiss was special. Not something that happened in front of a fake minister and a bunch of haystacks with boys chanting in the background, "Snog! Snog! Snog!" because it was their new favorite word.

Juni told him they should have a code word for when they were both ready. After negotiating, where Mason suggested *la bise* because it was French and romantic, they finally settled on something simple: *okay*.

Juni had been thinking about it since the dance, through Connor's vanishing and the dry heat of summer. Would today be the day she had her first kiss?

Or today?

Or maybe today?

And yet, how could she forget Connor for even a moment? Because when she was thinking about kissing, she definitely wasn't thinking about Connor.

THE NEXT DAY, Juni walked across her yard and up the Wheelers' front porch steps, which tilted a bit to the left. When she opened the heavy door, she faced herself in a giant gilded mirror that hung inside the foyer.

"Mirror, mirror, on the wall . . ." Juni said as she pressed down the temperamental waves of her dark hair.

Mason stood in the viewing room and gave her a small smile as she walked in, a single dimple on his left cheek. Gabby stood beside her older brother, Luca, Connor's best friend, who Juni was avoiding like he was made of spiders. Together, they were looking down at the tiniest casket Juni had ever seen.

Gabby's long walnut-colored ponytail hung flat against her back, and Luca's arm was around her shoulder, which gave Juni a heart pang. Because of course it did. It was bad enough that Juni had to see Luca be a big brother every day. But even worse was that he'd been with the army man and Father Thomas to notify Juni's family that Connor had gone missing. She tried to tell herself it wasn't Luca's fault, he'd only been there to help, but each time she saw him, she couldn't help but think about that terrible day.

Juni nudged Luca out of the way, a little harder than she needed to. This was the best friend's job, and she was late.

Gabby took her hand and held it tight.

Mason's dad, Mr. Wheeler, walked into the viewing room wearing his customary black suit of mourning, a stethoscope around his shoulders. He had a full head of salt-and-pepper hair, heavy on the salt, and a face full of freckles, just like most of the other Wheelers whose portraits hung in a straight line down the front hallway. Mason looked just like his dad and had already found his first gray hair this summer. He'd pulled it out and placed it in a red velvet box and showed it to Juni as though it were a mystical object.

"I'm so sorry, Gabby. I wanted to come and give you my condolences. I sure would love having one of Piper's paintings for my office."

Gabby used to dip Piper's tiny paws into Juni's paint and let her scurry around on a canvas, over and over again, an explosion of tiny dots. Rat-paw pointillism.

"Sure, Mr. W. I'll pick out the most colorful one." Then Gabby burst into tears, and Mr. Wheeler hugged her until a cow mooed out front—his next patient, most likely—so he excused himself.

Gabby wiped her eyes and touched Luca's arm. "Can you carry her?"

They moved single file along the flagstone path in the shade of the oaks and cedars. Eventually, Luca laid the casket into the small hole Mason had already prepared. The morning was hot and still, and there was a heavy smell of overturned earth. Juni tied her hair up in a ponytail to cool off the back of her neck.

Gabby cleared her throat. "You were a loyal friend and so very smart. You didn't turn your wheel at night, and you always pooped in your litter. You were a wonderful artist, and I will never forget you."

Juni read the headstone Mrs. Wheeler had carved:

HERE LIES PIPER
Tiny in Stature, But Large of Heart
A True Friend

"See the vegetable carvings?" Mason said. "I told Mom those were Piper's favorites. English peas, corn, romaine lettuce. The romaine was especially hard to carve." Mason puffed up as though he'd done it himself, and Gabby smiled, leaning down to trace a finger along the edges of the leaves.

"Goodbye, Piper," Gabby whispered.

She took Luca by the arm, and they walked toward the shaded patio and the peach cobbler Mrs. Wheeler had set on the table, while Juni and Mason grabbed their shovels to finish the job of burying Piper's casket. A thin ray of sunshine lit up Mason's coal-black hair, and Juni noticed small beads of sweat across the top of his lip. She wondered if kissing him would be salty.

A delicate breeze grew out of the summer-day stillness, and Juni took a deep, calming breath turning herself toward the lake. But the next breeze didn't come off the lake. It blew, instead, along the fine hairs at the back of her neck. She felt a pulling sensation, a beckoning that came from the woods behind her.

Juniper. A whisper. Or maybe it was the rustling leaves. Everything seemed to happen in slow motion after that.

Juni looked first at Mason, who hadn't seemed to hear the soft calling of her name as he kept shoveling. She slowly turned all the way around, and there, standing under the tire-swing oak across Last Chance Creek, was a large buck, his cupped ears turning side to side.

Juni felt the pace of her heart quicken. Goose bumps

prickled across her shoulders. Because it looked to Juni as though the buck from Connor's painting had stepped right off the mural hanging on her wall. She counted ten points, tattered bits of velvet still clinging to his antlers from their late-spring growth. Even his stance was the same.

Juni blinked to make sure she wasn't imagining things. She wanted to call to Mason so he could see what she was seeing, but her voice wouldn't work.

The buck dipped his great head and Juni suddenly knew, in the Grimm part of her heart, maybe, that somehow, impossibly, this glorious animal had been sent by her brother. She felt Connor all around her in that moment, intense and dazzling, like late-afternoon sunlight reflecting off the lake. She leaned against the tree as the pure agony of missing him rushed through her.

"Juni?" Mason said. "You okay?"

And just like that, the buck was gone, off into the woods in two graceful leaps.

"Did you see that?" Juni asked.

Mason looked over his shoulder in the direction of the tire swing. "See what?"

"The buck. Over there." She pointed toward the trees.

"Missed it," he said.

Juni closed her eyes and tried to soak in the feeling of her brother, that bright flash of light, as she helped Mason scoop the last of the dirt into Piper's tiny grave. She wondered if this was what going crazy felt like.

WHEN MASON AND Juni were finished shoveling, Mason linked their arms. He smelled like cinnamon toast. His eyes were a strange combination of brown, green and blue, like a mood ring, and when he looked at her, Juni could feel every bit of herself all at once. Like she was on fire or her skin was suddenly made of fine-grit sandpaper. She tried to push away the buck and the *where is he where is he where is he* thoughts, if only for a little while.

Mrs. Wheeler scooped healthy servings of peach cobbler into their bowls and cooed loving words to Gabby. She had such lovely hands, which Juni had drawn a hundred times without her knowing. Juni also liked to draw the long waves of her ashy-blond Rapunzel hair, which Mrs. Wheeler wore in a loose knot on top of her head.

"Thanks for carving her favorite vegetables," Gabby said.

"Of course, my sweet. It was the least I could do."

After they ate for a while, silver spoons tapping against her best bone china, Mrs. Wheeler asked, "Are you all set for your campout next weekend?"

The campout. Connor and Luca started going when they were fourteen. They chose Domingo Springs because it was less than half a mile from the Pacific Crest Trail and attracted a lot of thru-hikers, the ones traveling from Mexico to Canada or vice versa. Connor and Luca had sworn to each other they would hike the trail when Connor got home, all 2,659 miles.

The boys liked to sit around the campfire and listen to stories about near-death bear encounters and fox-shaped ghost sightings and help themselves to the large bags of candy the hikers always offered. Each summer, Connor and Luca would buy supplies of packaged food, fresh baked goods and containers of water. Then they would walk parts of the trail and leave those little bundles for the hikers to find.

Trail magic, the hikers called it. Because they would often find those little bundles of the exact thing they needed—a roll of toilet paper, sugary fruit punch or an apple—just when they felt like giving up.

When Mason, Gabby and Juni turned ten, the boys took the trio along, and the five of them prepared for the long weekend by having a smaller version of a tamalada at Gabby and Luca's house. Up until then, the Tavares family had only made tamales for Christmas, but Connor had begged Mrs. Tavares that year and no one could turn down Connor for anything. Now it was tradition to make enough tamales to share with the hikers they camped with.

Juni hadn't yet been brave enough to tell Mason and Gabby she wasn't going, but today was the day.

"We're making tamales on Wednesday first thing, and then Mom is taking us to the store for the rest of what we need," Gabby said, her leg bouncing under the table. "Can you make more of this exact cobbler? I could eat a truckload."

"I will make all the cobbler you can eat. Just the three of you again this year? And Luca, of course. No room for more?"

"You make people hug trees when they're finished with yoga, Mom. No one wants to be friends with us." But Mason laughed when he said it.

"I'm not going," Juni blurted.

"What?" both Mason and Gabby said at the same time.

"I just . . . can't."

Mrs. Wheeler laid her hand on top of Juni's and squeezed.

"I thought you wanted to go," Gabby finally said.

"I did. I do. It's just that I need to be here . . . in case they find Connor."

Mason eventually broke the lingering silence. "I guess we'll just have to set up camp in your yard instead, Juni. Out past the goat pen on the lake." He looked at Gabby. "We'll try again next year, right, Gab?"

Gabby took a small section of her long ponytail and began weaving a braid. "Sure. We'll catch frogs instead of fish, and then set them free. Like old times."

Juni wondered how long it would take Gabby to give up on her. They'd been a team since kindergarten, but Juni could feel her slipping away.

"Any news on Elsie?" Luca said, scooping more cobbler for himself. Juni was grateful for the change in subject, even if it was Luca.

"Still waiting," Juni said.

"Have you tried a PowerPoint presentation with all the relevant facts?" Gabby said. "Works every time."

"It's not her mom and dad. It's the army," Mason said.

But Juni wondered. Mom was so shifty when the subject came up. Like she knew something Juni didn't.

"Tell your mom and dad I'll stop by tomorrow and run the car," Luca said. He'd been taking care of Connor's restored Caprice station wagon as though it were Connor himself. "I'll see if I can sneak in a question about Elsie."

Juni looked toward the tire-swing oak, felt pulled to stand where the buck had stood, a smooth-like-honey feeling moving through her chest. The opposite of buzzing bees.

So, after the peach cobbler and and an afternoon spent comforting her best friend, Juni skipped over the rocks in Last Chance Creek and gazed up through the branches of the tree she'd climbed with her brother too many times to count. Then she looked down.

At the base of the oak was the tip of an antler bone, about two inches long and nestled in the leaves. As though the buck she'd seen earlier had dropped it there for her to find.

She held the bone close to her heart, and a shimmering came over everything, a strange frequency Juni could feel deep inside herself. Like a dial had turned the tiniest bit, and now she was receiving a clear signal from Connor, even if she didn't know what it meant.

None of this was strange for Juni. She had grown up believing in the deepest part of her heart, if not her logical mind, that if she just looked hard enough in all the creeks and rivers and the lake itself, she might find a wish-granting trout. Or if she captured a golden snake, she'd understand the language of animals. She believed in talking birds and enchanted flowers and singing bones.

Her own birth had been a miracle, so how could she not believe?

"Sing, little bone," she commanded. "Tell me everything."

Unable or unwilling, the antler bone did not answer.

THE LETTER
AND THE MEMORY DREAM

LATER THE NEXT afternoon, when Juni found out the foster family was coming for Penelope, her breathing turned thick with bees. Mom made her blow into the peak flow meter three times before noon, and logged her sweatiness and "dull eyes" into the diary. She moved Juni from the green zone into the yellow zone and called Dr. Montgomery around two o'clock. Since monitoring Juni's breathing was the only thing bringing Mom out of her room from time to time now, Juni was less annoyed than she could have been.

"We can't keep them all, Juni. I'm really sorry," Anya said as she packed the last of Penelope's bag at the kitchen counter.

"I'm going to the goat pen," Juni said, and slipped

outside before Mom was off the phone. She knew resting was in her future, but she needed some fresh air before that happened.

At least the family coming for Penelope was friendly. There was a very tall woman, a very short man, and two boys around Juni's age who looked like they might be twins, but not quite. This would be the second time they'd visited from Quincy, about an hour away.

Eventually, even from out in the goat pen, Juni heard them coming. Their laughter filled the front yard, the sky, the woods. Juni knew Penelope would be played with and snuggled and kept safe, and maybe she'd only scratch them accidentally. She was a bit ornery, that Penelope, and it had taken time for Juni to learn her moods. Penelope had returned the favor, always showing up just when Juni needed a warm fluff of comfort.

"You'd better go on and help," Dad said, letting himself into the pen. He grabbed a rake for the goat berries. "You know Penelope will only come out of hiding for you."

Dad's head was perfectly round and shiny and had freckle splotches that Juni had liked to connect with a dry erase pen when she was little. He used to take up all sorts of cheerful space, singing, "Heigh-ho! Heigh-ho! It's off to work, I go!" as he put on his baseball cap in the mornings. He used to tie fishing lures at the breakfast table, which caught him fairy-tale-sized fish and stories to match. His voice used to boom across the house, the yard, the world.

Calling her his June Bug. His Juni Bean.

"I'd rather stay here," Juni said. It might be the only time she got to spend with Dad that day, maybe even the next few days because if he wasn't roaming the woods, he was working as a handyman all over town. Dad worked weekends, too, doing what he could since losing his job at the Collins Pine Sawmill two years before.

But it wasn't only that. Juni just couldn't face losing something today.

After a minute or two, when Juni still hadn't left, Dad stopped, arms crossed on top of his rake, and stared at her, like he was about to growl an angry-bear growl.

She sighed and put hers away, leaving Dad to his lonely work.

Juni found everyone settled in the front room.

"Can you grab a contract?" Anya said to Juni. "We've already fetched Penelope from her hidey-hole."

"We've decided to name her Yolanda," one of the boys said, peering into the cat carrier. His bangs were short and uneven. "I like shouting, YO-LAN-DAAAAA!"

Juni sighed again and let herself into Anya's office. The desk was the usual mess of bills, coupon clippings and unread magazines. Juni moved things around looking for the folder marked Contracts. In the process, she tipped over a stack of magazines, and a manila folder slid to the floor.

The folder was marked Elsie.

Juni grabbed it. Inside were letters from a place called Service Dogs, with Love. Juni read through every letter and couldn't believe it. The last one especially. It was dated two weeks earlier.

Leonard McLaughlin
Service Dogs, with Love
PO Box 197
Arlington, TX 76001

Dear Mr. and Mrs. Creedy,

I was so sorry to hear of your final decision about Elsie. As I said, there is another family in Mammoth Lakes who are happy to take her. Captain Johnny Wilder served alongside Elsie prior to Connor, and he was honored to have the opportunity to bring her into their home. He wanted me to mention that his home is always open to you for a visit with Elsie if you'd like. Rest assured, she will be cared for and loved.

He's given me permission to give you his address and email.

John and Amanda Wilder
2629 Scrimshaw Lane
Mammoth Lakes, California
Johnnywilder60@usmail.com

Sincerely,

Leonard

"What's taking so long?" Anya said as she walked in.

Juni turned to look at her with the letters in one hand, the folder in the other. She began to wheeze.

Anya's eyes grew wide. "Juni, I . . ."

But Juni didn't want to hear anything she had to say. Maybe ever again. She rushed out of the office, angry thoughts crashing through her head. Mom and Dad had lied to her. But the fact that Anya knew and didn't say anything was worse.

Juni stormed past the family sitting on the worn living room couch as they chattered happily.

Anya followed her to the foot of the stairs. "Juni, please, let me explain."

Juni turned around and rasped, "How could you let them give away Connor's dog?"

"Juni . . ."

"I will *never* speak to you again."

Because of course she wouldn't. They were traitors.

Anya winced, like she'd caught her finger in a drawer. The Quincy family had fallen silent.

Juni wasn't sure how, or if, she could ever forgive them.

And then she stopped breathing altogether.

WHENEVER JUNI HAD an asthma attack, she'd have funny dreams afterward. Because they were part memory, part dream, she called them her memory dreams. This one was about Connor.

It had been raining the day he told Juni he'd joined the army. She sat on her bed while he explained that he'd been accepted into the canine program and was leaving for training at Lackland Air Force Base in Texas in ten days' time. All branches of the military trained with canines at Lackland.

It felt like a punch to the stomach, and Juni's bees swarmed her breath away.

"Should I get the bee smoker?" Connor said.

"No. I'm going to let myself suffocate and die and then it will be your fault," Juni said.

"I have to go, Juni. It's a good way to go to college. I'll be doing what I love while I figure out what I want to study. Like Anya says, 'Never turn down a quest.'"

"But you'll be questing in a dangerous place! There will be bombs and bad guys!"

"There are very few bad guys over there. Mostly good guys. I'll be safer than safe with a trained dog by my side."

But Juni didn't believe him. She took a puff from her inhaler.

Connor pulled Juni under the dining room table where he had taped butcher paper to the underside. He explained that they were going to paint a mural flat on their backs, the way Michelangelo had painted the ceiling of the Sistine Chapel.

They painted different scenes from their life and from the fairy tales. A gingerbread house. A catfish swimming through the pines at the bottom of the lake. Juni painted the juniper tree for which she was named, and Connor painted a wide-chested ten-point buck. The one who'd shadowed them on the day she was born.

When the painting was dry, they taped it to Juni's wall. They lay side by side on the floor and gazed at their creation while rain tapped the window.

"This way, you can look at the mural and remember I'm always with you."

"That's dorky."

"Yeah, well. At least I didn't say I'll be watching you because I've found a way to look out through the painting, like a magic mirror."

"That's creepy, not dorky."

They were quiet for a while, heads touching.

"You'll be on a quest yourself while I'm gone," Connor said.

"How?"

"You'll have to find a way to live without me." A joke, but it was truer than true.

Then he said, "You've got this, Juni. You're stronger than you think you are."

"I can't even breathe right."

Connor pointed to their painting. "That buck lived long enough to grow ten points. He avoided disease and bullets and pack animals. That's what I want you to think about when you look at him. He was a survivor and so are you. I'll be back before you know it."

Even then, Juni felt the lie snake-wrap itself around her chest. He would be gone for an entire year, and a year was forever.

Turns out a year wasn't forever.

Every moment—when someone you love is missing—is forever.

NEVER TURN DOWN A QUEST

THE ASTHMA ATTACK had been sudden. Dizzy, Juni had knocked her head on a wooden step when she fell. Because of Anya's panicked yelling, Dad had rushed in from the goat pen and carried Juni into her room, where Mom fluttered around her bed. Dad talked softly, the way Connor used to, his hand on her belly, where her diaphragm struggled underneath.

Think about the bee smoker, Juni.

The way it quiets the bees.

Quiet and still.

Dad said the words over and over, *quiet and still.* Connor's words. Then, she slept.

When she woke from her memory dream a few hours later, something Connor had said niggled at her, but she couldn't pin it down. Was it the part about survival? Or that he'd be watching out for her? The memory faded the way dreams do.

Juni turned on her side and looked at the antler bone she'd found the day before. She'd set it on her nightstand so it would be near her when she slept, working its way into her dreams, maybe, to give her answers. She touched it softly with one finger, and there it was again, that feeling of a radio signal coming in clear and true.

"What are you trying to tell me?"

Juni got up and stretched, crossing to the picture window that looked out onto their grassy meadow, thick woods beyond. The sun had long since gone down, and the sky was a deep-sea blue, not yet full dark. In the distance past the trees, even though she couldn't see it, was Mount Lassen, which had exploded into an ashy landslide a hundred years back. Connor had hiked all over Lassen National Forest, said he could feel the rumbling promise of another eruption deep in the earth beneath his feet. Juni could feel it, too, had felt it all her life in her dreams, but didn't think it was the volcano. Her dream rumbling took the form of giants stomping through her meadow, or tower-sized pines crashing to the forest floor. She dreamed of six-foot ravens nesting in the oak outside her window, their wing beats matching the rhythm of her heart. Juni often felt as though her room was the center of a snow globe, a fairy-tale world living just outside the glass.

It had been Anya's room, after all. Perhaps the magic had spun from her dreams when she was a young girl so many years ago.

Great-Grandmother Abigail had decorated Anya's room in soft colors. There was the original wallpaper with tiny lavender and butter-yellow flowers, and curtains made from sturdy rose gingham that Anya took down in the spring and autumn, washed by hand, and hung to dry in the meadow. The curtains were threadbare in places, but Juni would never part with them. It would be like parting with Anya herself.

Unbearable.

Just like Anya's betrayal.

Feeling the urge to draw antlers again, Juni reached for a brown marker on her desk and began to draw a wide set in the middle of her picture window.

There was a knock at the door. Anya poked her head in. "You missed dinner," she said. She carried a plate of pale chicken and roasted broccoli spears.

"I want to be alone."

Anya sat on the edge of Juni's bed as she finished drawing. It didn't take long. She drew them uneven, one side higher than the other, a simple outline. If she squinted, it looked as though the oak tree outside her window had a wide set of antlers growing among its branches.

"I'm not hungry, Anya."

"I came here to say some things and I'm not leaving until I do."

Juni sat, and Anya set the plate of chicken on her lap. "I know what it feels like to lose a brother. Your parents do not."

"What does that have to do with Elsie?"

Anya brushed a wispy wave from Juni's eye. "Don't you understand?"

"What is there to understand? Connor said she was ours. She's family. And you gave her away."

"Seeing Elsie would be a reminder. Every single day."

"Why wouldn't they want to be reminded of Connor? He's still out there!"

"Elsie came home, Juni. She came home and Connor didn't."

Juni considered this. "Why didn't they just tell me, then? I'm not a baby."

"Your father was hoping your mom might change her mind."

It was all too much. Juni was suddenly tired. Sleeping-spell tired. She set the dinner plate on her nightstand beside the bone and lay down, closing her eyes. Maybe she'd started dreaming the moment she felt antlers sprout from her head all those days ago, and hadn't woken up yet.

A moment later, Anya gasped, and Juni sat up, startled. Anya held the antler bone with an exaggerated look of surprise, as though she'd just watched it grow from her very own palm. "Where did you get this?"

"Do you think it means something?" Juni said, suddenly wide awake. "I found it in the pet cemetery."

Anya's eyes were extraordinarily blue. Blue like a wish-granting sapphire, or the deepest part of an enchanted sea. She stared past Juni, past the walls of Juni's room, past Mount Lassen and the sky beyond, maybe. A full minute ticked by, two. Juni waited, hoping she would answer the question.

"Mama had one just like this. It was a protection charm. She wore it everywhere. Luck against the curse was what she always said. It had been in our family for generations."

Juni became very still. A tear rolled down Anya's cheek, and Juni whispered, "Please, Anya. I need to know."

Anya set the antler bone back on the nightstand and walked around to the other side of the bed, where she settled in against Juni's cotton pillows. Juni could smell the lavender on Anya's hands from working in the garden.

Juni waited as Anya took a deep breath.

"Fairy tales are alive. That was what the Grimms believed. They thought of the stories as a part of nature, untamed as a wolf, wild as a grove of trees or a mountain stream. And as a story traveled, mouth to ear, mouth to ear, like a game of Telephone, it always came back changed, the tellers becoming part of the telling. In that way, our own family legend is itself like a fairy tale.

"The trick is finding where you begin and the story ends." Anya paused and turned toward Juni as though she were having second thoughts. "I haven't wanted to talk about this. I worry that saying a thing out loud can draw the attention of the fates. As long as we don't catch their eye, we are safe."

Juni knew exactly what Anya meant because Juni herself had always felt she'd cheated Death, and deep down believed he'd never give up looking for her.

"The fates will do what they will do, I suppose. Perhaps the thing to remember is that we are in charge of how we respond." She nodded one time, as though she'd made a decision. "Where should I start?"

"At the beginning," Juni said.

Anya pointed to Juni's book on her nightstand, *The Original Folk & Fairy Tales of the Brothers Grimm*, and Juni handed it to her. Anya settled it on her lap.

"There were many along the way who contributed to the Grimm Brothers' collection, but some stories they stole.

"A handful came from a Greek woman who lived deep in the Tharandt Forest near Dresden, but which ones they were have been lost to time. What is known for certain is that Jacob and Wilhelm had visited this woman themselves, and a bargain was struck.

"They were supposed to retrieve something precious to her, something sacred that had been stolen. Some said it was an object. Some said it was a child. Whatever it was, Jacob and Wilhelm couldn't or wouldn't retrieve it, and the rest you know. She cursed them and all their family to suffer through versions of their beloved fairy tales."

"There must be a way to break the curse, though," Juni said. "There's always a way to break a curse."

Anya placed her hands flat against the cover of the book. "If there is, it didn't come down with the family legend."

Juni thought about the many ways to break a curse that were written into the fairy tales themselves. Getting a magic spell from a witch. Sacrificing something cherished. Going on a quest for a magical object. This stopped Juni in her tracks.

An idea began to take shape.

"But there have been other miracles besides mine. It's not just doom and gloom."

"Fairy tales are filled with horrors, but they are filled with miracles, too, and our family has had its share. Remember the story of Great-Uncle Clive, who was struck by ball lightning but survived and went on to live to one hundred and four? And your great-great-grandmother Holle was a diviner, finding not just water, but lost objects. There are so many others."

Anya took Juni's hand. "On my good days, I feel as though these are stories you might find in anyone's family tree. On my bad days, the curse feels true."

"What happened to the lucky antler bone? The one your mom wore?"

"I lost it. Which is why I ran away from Teddy and Abigail. It was a quest of sorts, but that is a story for another day."

"Never turn down a quest," Juni said. It's what Connor had told her, what she'd been trying to remember from her memory dream.

Anya kissed the back of Juni's hand and let it go. She pointed to the chicken dinner. "Eat. You need your strength." She set *The Original Folk & Fairy Tales of the Brothers Grimm* on the bed where she'd been sitting, and then she left.

Anya wasn't like most of her friends' grandmas, with

their holiday sweaters and persistent baking. Anya was more likely to dance around a bonfire and speak to the birds than she was to pull a hankie out of her bra, like Luca and Gabby's abuela did. Anya didn't have many friends, preferring the company of her family or to be alone. She was known to dye her hair with the change of seasons—magenta for fall and indigo for summer. She made jewelry from precious stones, and went for walks through the woods in the full moonlight, her trusty stick her only companion. She was the reason Juni believed in the power of stories.

Juni stared at Connor's buck and let the memories wash over her. The way they used to argue over the last scoop of ice cream in the carton, or the right way to roll the toothpaste tube. How she took his sweatshirts without asking. She thought about sleeping in Connor's room under the giant carved desk that once belonged to Grandpa Charlie, the terrible smell of socks drifting from his closet. She thought about hanging pine-tree air fresheners in his room and how he'd put his favorite books under her pillow and the many times he'd told her the story of how he'd saved her life once upon a time.

She needed to hear it told again.

Because even though Anya had surrounded her with stories since birth, Juni believed in miracles because of Connor.

Never turn down a quest, Anya had always said.

This was the answer. This had always been the answer.

Juni had to go get Elsie. She had to fashion herself a quest to break the curse, and maybe, just maybe, she could create a miracle and Connor could come home. Because fairy tales were filled with horrors, but they were filled with miracles, too.

Connor had always been the hero of their story.

Now, ready or not, it was Juni's turn.

A HAYSTACK SECRET

THE IDEA BLOOMED overnight like one of Anya's windowsill orchids.

Juni would take herself on a quest, because of course she would.

And because there was no time to lose, she started planning right after breakfast.

First, she read through every quest story she could remember from *The Original Folk & Fairy Tales from the Brothers Grimm*—Jorinde and Joringel, Hansel and Gretel, Little Brother, Little Sister—then she skimmed through the rest to make sure she hadn't missed any. It took her most of the morning, but when she finished, she had a list of tasks.

With an endless number to choose from, Juni settled

on the three that repeated the most, otherwise she'd be questing for the rest of her life.

Return a stolen object to its rightful owner.

Find a witch and ask for a magic spell.

Sacrifice something cherished.

Although she had no idea what might pass for a witch in California in the twenty-first century, or how she might get a magic spell from such a person, the other two were easier to consider. She'd go retrieve the stolen Elsie, and since the sacrifice didn't usually come until the end of the fairy tale, she had time to figure that part out.

Next, she went to her computer and clicked open the internet, searching the word *witches*. All sorts of interesting information came up. She read the wiki and a couple of articles in *Time* and the *New York Times*. Turns out people still practiced witchcraft in many different and interesting ways. Green and herbalist witches, or forest witches, used the power of plants and trees to spin their magic. Just like Gabby and Luca's mom did with the herbal remedies she grew in her garden.

So, remembering their vacation to San Francisco last year, when Mom had typed *best doughnuts near me* into her phone, Juni typed *witches near me* into her computer, and bingo. There were witch groups and divining witches—like Great-Great-Grandmother Holle—and psychics who called themselves witches. Although they weren't exactly everywhere, Juni found a witch in Meadow Valley near Quincy, at Madame Ophelia's Crystal Emporium. It was a place to start, anyway.

The last thing she did was print out a map from the internet. There were a few different ways to get from her home in Chester to Elsie in Mammoth Lakes, and one of them was Highway 89. It wound its way through national forest land; Lassen, Plumas, Tahoe, Eldorado, Stanislaus and finally, the Inyo National Forest. If they stayed on 89, they'd never have to leave the woods.

Because all proper quests happened in the woods.

Juni opened her nightstand drawer and lifted out the heart-shaped chocolate box Mason had given her last year on Valentine's Day. Inside she kept her most treasured possessions, each of which smelled like chocolate. A story she'd torn from Anya's *Reader's Digest* called "The Lake," a perfectly round wishing stone from Last Chance Creek, a haiku of Mason's that Juni had snuck out of the school garbage can, and Connor's letters from basic training and Afghanistan.

Specifically, she wanted to read one of the first he'd sent.

Dear Juni,

It won't be long now before I'm finished with training. I was assigned a dog named Elsie. She's a golden retriever named for 2nd Lt. Elsie S. Ott, a flight nurse on the first intercontinental air evacuation flight ever, during World War II. Normally, men were evacuated on ships, which took three months to get home to the United States. Flying was dangerous, but faster, and so, after this first successful voyage, where Elsie took care of five men, she was asked both how to evacuate more safely and what was needed to make these flights more comfortable. Most of the items she listed were for the wounded—oxygen, more bandages, extra coffee—but she also said wearing a skirt was highly impractical and that she would be wearing pants from then on, whether they liked it or not.

Two months later, Elsie Ott received the U.S. Air Medal, the first given to a woman in the U.S. Army.

Elsie's story made me think of you, Juni. I love thinking about you out there in the world, how much better it is for having you in it. Will you show your art in a gallery one day? Design buildings? Build schools on another continent? Illustrate children's books? I can't wait to see.

They named this dog for a hero, and she lives up to that responsibility every single day. I don't know what I'd do without her. It's like having four eyes instead of two, two sets of instincts instead of one. We share the same heart.

She's ours now, Juni. She's family.

Give Anya, Mom and Dad hugs, and punch Luca in the arm. Tell him I said to "eat worms." He'll know what that means.

Love until my next letter,

Connor

Juni held the picture of Elsie that Connor had sent in the letter. Connor was on one knee, Elsie smiling at him like he was the best thing that ever happened to her.

That Elsie was a golden retriever sent a shimmy across Juni's shoulders. Golden animals were everywhere in the fairy tales, and often the object of a quest. Juni jumped up and did a little dance. She'd finally figured it out.

For the first time since Connor had vanished, Juni knew exactly what to do. Instead of their camping trip to Domingo Springs, she would persuade Mason, Gabby and Luca to drive with her to Mammoth instead, where Elsie had been sent.

But just as suddenly as those happy feelings came, they vanished. As she calculated the distance to Mammoth Lakes—exactly 286.7 miles—doubt crept in.

You're fragile, Juni. Try to remember that.

Her mother's words were a web in her brain, set to trap everything else.

Juni knew how preposterous this might seem. Believing she was cursed. Believing a quest would bring her brother back to her. Was there enough evidence, gathered over the generations of her family, to prove any of this could possibly be true? Juni didn't know.

But one thing she did know: If there was even the tiniest sliver of a little bit of a possibility, didn't Juni owe it to her brother to try?

SINCE JUNI ONLY had a couple of days to talk her friends into helping, she called an emergency goat-pen meeting, trying her best to ignore the web of doubt. She asked Gabby and Mason to come first so she could explain her plan, and then asked Luca to come a half hour later. That way all three of them could talk him into it.

Maybe she could forgive Luca for delivering the worst news of her life if he did this for her.

When Gabby and Mason arrived, they sat on the scraggly bales of hay they'd pushed into a circle. It was where they'd always had their most important discussions. Like planning Gabby's eighth-grade presidential campaign for next year, or that time they'd decided to run away with the county-fair carnival crew so they'd never have to eat kale again.

Juni had packed everything—the letter from Service Dogs, with Love, the photo Connor had sent of himself with Elsie and the letter Connor had written about her—into a manila envelope. She took each item out, one by one, and gave them to her friends.

"Okay. What I'm about to tell you is a Haystack Secret. It doesn't leave the goat pen."

"Of course not," Gabby said. She immediately started braiding a section of her long ponytail, knee bouncing.

Juni took a deep breath. "First off, I just found out Mom and Dad let Elsie go to another family."

"What happened?" Mason said.

"It's all in these letters." Juni pulled them out of the envelope and handed them to her friends.

Gloria the goat sat on Juni's feet, being the sweet goat she was, and tucked her front legs beneath her. Juni scratched the coarse white fluff between her ears.

"She's in Mammoth?" Gabby finally said.

"Before you say anything, just think about it." Juni paused, gathering her courage from the goats, the hay bales, the woods. "We could drive to Mammoth to get Elsie instead of going on the camping trip."

After Gabby and Mason blinked so many times Juni began to wonder if they'd malfunctioned, Mason finally jumped up and one-two-punched the air. "Yes! A rescue operation!"

"But your parents must not want her or they wouldn't have let this happen," Gabby said. "How are you going to change their minds?"

"I'm not going to tell them." Juni felt guilty even as she said it. "It's not like they would send her back. They aren't monsters. They're just sad."

"What if this other family won't let her go?" Gabby said.

"Whose side are you on, anyway?" Juni said.

"Of course I'm on your side. This just seems . . . next level."

Juni wanted to tell them how Connor's and Elsie's fates might be intertwined, how her feeling of purpose in going on this quest had become overwhelming. Mason and Gabby both knew about the Grimm family legend, the same way they knew the story of Izzy the German shepherd. But maybe it was one thing to tell odd stories and another to believe them.

So, instead of saying anything about quests or antler bones or fate, Juni rubbed a piece of hay between her fingers and brought it to her nose, the sweet smell of summer setting her thoughts in a proper line. "Connor would have done this for me. For any of us. Elsie is family, and I need your help."

Juni spied Luca walking toward them from the lake trail. He was tall, over six feet, thin and muscular, his veins showing on his biceps and the backs of his hands. He was studying to be an emergency medical technician and knew how to perform CPR and the Heimlich maneuver, as well as fashion a tourniquet, and an assortment of other lifesaving techniques. Juni knew they'd be safe with Luca.

He reached the goat pen and let himself in. Luca's eyes were brown like Gabby's, the color of cedar bark. "Okay, guys, what's all this about?"

Juni looked at Gabby and Mason.

"I say yes," Mason said.

Gabby tossed her hands up in surrender. "Fine!"

A breeze worked its way from one tree to the next, as though one of Juni's dream giants had just walked past, trailing a hand through the leaves. She faced Luca. "What if we went camping somewhere else?"

EATING WORMS

"NO WAY," LUCA said.

"But you haven't even thought about it! It's not that far. We aren't leaving the state or anything. And we could take Connor's Caprice!" Juni said. "It runs like a dream. Even you said so."

"It's not about reliable transportation, Juni. Your parents would kill me. Mason's parents would kill me. My own parents would kill me. I'd be dead three times over."

"Which is why we aren't going to tell them."

Luca had nudged in beside his sister on the hay bale. He sat forward, arms resting on his thighs, twisting a single bent piece of hay between his fingers around and around. "Look, this sucks," he said. "I can't believe your parents did this. But there is no way I'm going to go against what they want. They'll never trust me again. Did you even think about that? This isn't like you, Juni."

How could Juni have ever thought Luca would agree? Connor had been the one to throw himself off waterfalls and plan a thru-hike on the Pacific Crest Trail and join the army. He was the hero of the story. Luca was the sidekick.

"I'll go on my own. You can't stop me."

Gabby's heel bounced in the hay, making a shush, shush, shushing sound, and had twisted her hair into so many braids, Juni wondered how she'd get them all out. Mason leaned back on his long arms and stared off into space.

They'd given up.

What came next could only be described as pure desperation. For one clear moment, Juni didn't worry about what Gabby might think, how the story might sound, or if saying it out loud might force her to face the impossibility of it all.

"I think Connor is trying to tell me something."

Luca tied a blue bandanna over his short hair and stared her right in the eye. Gabby and Mason sat very still.

"What do you mean?" Luca said.

It was all she had left. Her only way to get Luca to understand.

So, Juni explained what she'd seen in the pet cemetery. She told them about the buck, who seemed to have stepped off the mural from her wall. How she'd found the antler bone, right where the buck had stood, and the shimmery feeling of Connor that came with it.

She kept the curse part to herself. How this quest would help her break it.

"It has to mean something, right?" Juni said.

Gabby didn't look as doubtful as Juni had feared.

Luca smiled. "I had a dream about Connor last night," he said. "It was about this thing that happened when we were kids."

Luca showed them a small wrist tattoo. It was an inch-worm. Juni hadn't noticed it before.

"We were ten, and Connor dug up this worm in Ma's herb garden. He told me it had magical powers and said if I ate it, I'd be magical, too. Of course, I ate it, because Connor would never lie to me, right? He got so mad! He said now he'd have to eat one too or it wouldn't be honorable. He didn't think I'd do it.

"We used to tell each other, 'Eat worms,' before we'd do something hard, or take a chance. Before a big test, or asking a girl on a date. It's the last thing I said to him before he left for basic."

"Look!" Juni jumped up and grabbed the envelope from where it sat beside Mason. She gave him Connor's letter. "Remember? He wrote about that in his first letter."

"Maybe he's trying to tell you something, too, Luca," Mason said.

"We have to go get Elsie. She's family," Juni said again.

Luca stood, hands on lean hips, and stretched. He grabbed a rake. "Let me think about it."

Juni stood and wiped the hay off her backside. The tops of her thighs were turning pink.

"Listen, Juni, if I can make this happen, you aren't to ask any questions. Got it? My methods are my own and you will do exactly what I tell you."

"Fine."

"And if I can't, you need to promise you won't try to go by yourself. Getting a bus ticket or whatever. Your parents would never get over it."

But Juni wasn't so sure. Connor was the light and the laughter of their lives, while Juni was the midnight trip to the emergency room. The number on the peak flow meter.

"Okay, I guess."

"Well, go on! I'm thinking," Luca said. He began Juni's

job of cleaning up the goat berries, and they left him to it.

As Juni trudged through the weedy ricegrass toward the house—Gabby on one side, Mason on the other—she decided that if Luca said no, she would find her own way.

Because of course she would.

WILD THINGS

FOUR DAYS HAD passed with no word from Luca, so Juni was in the process of freaking out. It was already Tuesday, and the campout was supposed to start on Thursday. Juni was certain she'd lose her mind before then.

Her alarm went off at 6:20, like it did every morning, waking her from a dream where she wore a dress made of paper and followed a trail of feathers deep into the woods. As though the curse had slithered into her dreams.

Juni pulled on jean shorts and yesterday's T-shirt and crept downstairs, avoiding the squeaky places in the floorboards so she wouldn't wake Mom. She only had a couple of minutes to get to the Caprice or she'd miss it.

Just before he left for basic training, Connor lost his watch in his car, a 1968 turquoise Chevy Caprice station wagon with wood paneling. And every morning at 6:35—the time Connor used to get up to swim before heading down the hill to his junior college classes at Feather River, or his job at the Sports Nut—the watch alarm went off. Juni liked to be there when it did.

The station wagon turned heads because it was in such great condition for being so old, and probably because it was turquoise. Connor had loved the attention, talking with other car lovers about where he'd found the original metallic vinyl upholstery for the seats, and how long it had taken to get a complete set of matching metal hubcaps. Don't even get him started on the Tripoli Turquoise paint and how he'd hunted down the formula so it was exactly the same as the paint they'd used in 1968.

Connor was a tinkerer, a person who could look at something mechanical and know exactly how it worked. He was that way with people, too, knowing what to say, what to do, to make a person feel like a million bucks.

Juni opened the driver's side of the Caprice, the vinyl seat cool against her legs as she slid in, and saw a folded piece of paper on the dash above the steering wheel, with *Juni* written on top. She unfolded it.

We're on.
Luca

Juni was momentarily stunned. And then she lifted her arms in a V for victory.

Unexpectedly, the passenger door opened, and there, of all people, was Dad.

"Good morning," he said, and sat beside her. She dropped her arms and slid Luca's note under her leg.

The scent of woodsmoke and pinesap followed him into the car. Dad often woke in the middle of the night and walked through the woods until sunrise. Sometimes he sat inside a hollowed tree near the creek, setting small fires that cast dancing shadows onto the weeping cedars. Juni knew because she'd followed him.

Connor's watch went off just then, each muffled beep a stab to her heart. They sat through it quietly.

"Where do you suppose it is?" Dad said.

"I don't know. Sounds like it's coming from every-where."

It had happened last summer when Connor had taken the seats out for reupholstery. He'd ripped out the carpet underneath the floor mats, too, to replace it. Right after the seats had gone back in, he'd noticed his watch was missing. They'd looked all over the house and yard, in his toolbox and the garage. No luck.

Then one morning he went to work early for the Summerama Sale, and the alarm went off in the car while he was driving.

You'll never guess where I found the watch, Juni!

He didn't get a chance to take the car apart to find it before he left.

Juni and Dad watched together as the sky brightened all around them. To Juni, this time of morning felt like floating up from a deep, dark well. She had the urge to tell Dad about what was happening. About growing antlers, and the curse. About her quest for Elsie. Maybe she could reach him. Maybe he would go with her.

She used to tell him everything.

But then Juni remembered a time she'd been walking in the woods and came upon a deer and her fawn grazing the wild blackberry bushes along a rocky stream. Juni was only five feet away when they all saw one another and froze. Juni hadn't moved, overwhelmed by the unexpected need for them to trust her. To recognize her goodness. But it wasn't in the nature of wild things to stick around.

Juni had a similar feeling come over her now. If she made one wrong move, said one wrong thing, Dad would flee back into the woods.

But there was a story she needed to hear, and she wanted to hear it from Dad.

"Can you tell me about the day I was born?" Juni said.

After a little while, long enough for Juni to think it had been too much to ask, Dad started talking. Juni closed her eyes, trying hard to believe in the possibility of one more miracle.

IT HAD BEEN a hot September. Before Dad had lost his job at the mill, they still had their own house, which had been about a mile through the woods from Anya and Grandpa Charlie. When Mom had been pregnant with Juni, she used to take a walk every morning along Last Chance Creek, ending up at Anya's, the calm water soothing her worries. Because Mom wasn't supposed to have any more babies. There'd been trouble with Connor's birth, and Mom had almost died. Dr. Wanda had told her she was done. Too much damage on the inside had made another baby impossible.

But Juni happened anyway. That was the first miracle.

Mom took those walks to Anya's by herself, and on those walks, she talked to Juni about all sorts of things, always starting the conversation with "Did you know, my miraculous baby girl?"

But on this particular day, the day Juni was born, Mom had brought Connor along. She didn't know why. Usually this was her quiet time, a few minutes of peace she liked to gather before heading into her day. When asked, Mom had said she'd woken with Connor on her mind, thinking she'd like to take him along. There weren't many days left for just the two of them. Happily, Connor went.

About fifteen minutes into their walk, Mom felt a pain in her lower belly. Just the one. Then she felt an urge she remembered from giving birth to Connor. The overwhelming urge to push.

So right there, beside Last Chance Creek, Mom pushed once, twice, three times, and Juni was born into Connor's waiting arms. She was lifeless and gray as a river rock, and Mom worked hard to stay calm as she walked Connor through each step.

Take off your shoelace.

Tie it around the umbilical cord.

Take that sharp rock.

Cut just there.

And still, Juni wasn't breathing.

Mom placed Juni in Connor's arms, pulling the edge of his T-shirt around her tiny body. Hold her head. Hold her neck. And run. Fast. Run as fast as you can to Anya and Grandpa Charlie.

Connor didn't want to go, of course. Mom was pale, shaking. But his new sister was so tiny. Fragile. And she wasn't breathing. Mom told him she was fine. She could take care of herself. His sister needed him.

So Connor ran, tears falling on his new baby sister.

There was a flash of white off in the trees. The sound of hoofbeats.

It was a buck, running through the underbrush on the other side of the path, shadowing him step for step. Connor didn't know whether to be afraid or in awe, so he decided on both as he picked up speed.

And about halfway to Anya and Grandpa Charlie's house, as he passed through the cool shade of the only juniper tree in their woods, Connor said later, Juni took her first breath. He didn't know how he knew, but there was a shift in the forest. An unseasonal breeze had gathered. The juniper above him, the trees all around, seemed to sigh with relief.

The buck had vanished.

Connor said it was magic.

That was the second miracle.

Juni stayed in the hospital for six weeks. The doctors said they had done everything they could; the rest was up to her. She would either find the strength deep inside her tiny body, or she wouldn't.

She found the strength. That was the third miracle.

They'd written about Juni's birth in the *Chester Progressive*. "Brave in the Woods" was what they'd titled the article. The mayor had given Connor a medal for heroism. It was Connor who had named her Juniper, for the tree whose cool shade he'd passed through when she'd taken her first breath.

WHEN DAD STOPPED talking, there were tears on his cheeks.

"I'm sorry, Dad."

"There's nothing to apologize for," Dad said, and wiped the tears roughly with his palms. He reached into his back pocket and pulled out a cell phone. "Here. It was Connor's. They sent it with his personal effects. Much better than the Fireplug, or Dragonfly, or whatever it is that Mom makes you carry around. You're almost a teenager. Time for a teenager's phone."

Dad placed it in her hand. Juni hadn't known they'd sent Connor's things.

"No social media. Of any kind. This is strictly a communication device. Reception is bad most everywhere, anyway, but you'll figure it out."

Connor's smartphone had a new plastic cover. Purple, her favorite.

"About Elsie . . ." Dad started. "Mom and I . . . we just couldn't have her here."

"But how do you know? What if we'd gotten Elsie and

it was the very thing we needed most? What about when Connor comes back?"

Dad stared at a honeybee crawling across the hood of the car. "He's not coming back, Juni."

Juni had read that certain people couldn't live with the unknown, and their only way of coping was to believe the missing person was dead. She had never thought her own father would be one of those people.

"You don't know that," she said.

Dad opened the door. "He's gone, Juni. It's time you accepted that."

But she wouldn't accept it. Not ever. It was as though Connor and Juni had been fused in some magical way under the juniper tree, and Juni felt certain she would know if Connor was gone from this world.

Now she just had to prove to everyone that she was right.

ON BORROWED TIME

WEDNESDAY WAS TAMALE day. They gathered early on Gabby and Luca's deck, where Mr. and Mrs. Tavares cooked in the summer. A camping stove had been set up under the eaves where they boiled water and stewed the meat so the house stayed cool. Inside the house, Mr. Tavares set up stations with the hojas, masa, and stewed meat, and they all stood in an assembly line: Mr. and Mrs. Tavares, Mrs. Wheeler, Luca, Juni, Gabby and Mason. Mrs. Tavares put on the usual upbeat tamalada music; this time it was Chuck Berry and Buddy Holly.

In the past, Mr. Tavares would take Mrs. Tavares in his arms from time to time and swing-dance her around the table. She would shout at him, "¡Ándale! ¡Ponte a trabajar!" and laugh. There would be gossip and snacks and lots of critiquing of one another's work.

"You put in too much meat!"

"You didn't put in enough meat!"

But this year was serious, quiet.

In just under four hours, they had 103 tamales. The kids were supposed to take seventy-five for themselves and the hikers on the PCT. But they weren't going to Domingo Springs now, and even though they could never eat that many tamales on their own, they had to pack them or the parents might be suspicious. Luca said he'd figure something out, and that was the end of that.

Gabby looked miserable the whole time they put the tamales together. She had never once lied to her parents. Never once. Mr. Tavares had told them he would always know if they were lying. Un chile no le pica a los mentirosos. A chili pepper isn't hot to liars.

And although Juni wasn't quite as strict about the truth as Gabby—for example, she didn't report every last wheezy breath to Mom—this particular lie made the bees hum.

THE DAY OF the trip finally arrived, and just as Juni packed the last of her things into a duffel, including a map to Madame Ophelia's, Anya let herself into Juni's room.

She carried a thin leather book, its cover embossed with flowers.

"I believe it will help you to know what happened all those years ago." Anya sat on Juni's bed and patted the space beside her. Juni sat. "It's the first story I ever wrote, and it's about the time I came to live with Teddy and Abigail. It explains why I ran away."

There had always been an undercurrent inside of Anya, like the heavy flow of snowmelt from the Feather River rushing under the surface of Lake Almanor. A deep sadness that would sweep her away for hours, sometimes days, at a time. Juni had believed she'd never know why.

The small book felt heavier than it should as Juni took it into her hands. She knew the mysteries written in its pages were the cause of that undercurrent, and for a brief moment, Juni worried that uncovering Anya's dark secrets might pull her under, too.

And yet, it was the most precious thing anyone had ever given her. She wrapped her arms around her grandmother and they rocked back and forth, back and forth.

"Read it aloud," Anya said, sitting back. "It's good to reason things out with friends. There are lots of blank pages left. Use them for yourself. Sketch your antlers. Write about your trip. It helps."

"What trip? We're just going around the corner," Juni said, nervous.

Anya took Juni's cheek in her palm. "Don't be mad at Luca. He had to tell someone."

Juni closed her eyes. She should have known, of course. Luca was a disappointment in every way. "Are you going to tell Mom and Dad?"

"It wouldn't be right not to, but I'm going to give you a couple hours' head start," Anya said. "Certain things need doing, and I think I can help them understand that."

Juni calculated the odds of getting all the way to Mammoth now that her parents were about to find out what she'd done. She had no hope they'd do anything other than freak out and demand she come home. Without Elsie.

For the second time, Juni felt uncertain in her quest. What was the point of doing something this difficult if she was sure to fail? Even a two-hour head start wouldn't matter in the end.

Anya reached into her pants pocket and pulled out a thin black satin cord. "If you'd like, I can attach this to your antler. Then you can wear yours the way Mama did."

Juni handed her the small tip of the buck's antler and Anya wrapped a thin silver wire around the top, making a loop for the cord to pass through. She placed it over Juni's head so it lay flat against her chest. Juni took the whole thing into her palm and felt the shimmer of Connor again, like the tail end of a musical note, warm and resonant in her chest.

Maybe this feeling, this certainty, was all that mattered.

"Thank you," Juni whispered.

Anya touched the antler bone one last time. "Go get our girl."

EVEN THOUGH THE Wheeler family had Cheez Whiz money, the house could have used a fresh coat of blue paint and white trim. Plus, there was that little knobby thing at the top of the banister that was always falling off for no apparent reason. Because there were bite marks all over it from when Izzy the German shepherd used to knock it down and bury it in the yard, everyone said Izzy's ghost was there, still trying to play, which made the knob a good luck charm for the Wheelers. They'd never fix it, of course, and Mrs. Wheeler said that was why they didn't fix up the rest of the house, either. For continuity purposes.

They met in the Wheeler driveway at nine o'clock sharp, Gabby and Mason each shoving their packs through the back window of the station wagon. Mason looked slightly ill in his favorite green alien T-shirt—he wasn't a fan of lying, either—and Gabby already had about five thousand tiny braids in her hair, sticking out at odd angles. Juni was grateful for her friends and felt steadied by Anya's words: *Go get our girl.*

Dad wandered in from the woods and stood next to Mr. Wheeler with his stethoscope. Mr. Tavares walked over to join them and squeezed Dad's shoulder in his coachlike way. Mrs. Tavares and Mrs. Wheeler were bookends to Mom and Anya at the porch railing. They were one of the few reasons Mom left her room—to drink the tea they brought, or eat the cookies and pies they baked. Even if it was only a bite or two at a time.

As Juni leaned forward to slide her own pack into the back of the station wagon, the antler bone swung forward.

"Can I touch it?" Gabby said.

Juni held it out by the cord, and Gabby let it rest against her palm.

"It's warm," she said.

Juni wondered if Gabby had felt something more, though. Because Gabby suddenly let go of the antler bone and hurried to the front seat, rubbing at her palm.

The rest of them climbed in, too, and as Luca started the engine to let it warm, Mrs. Tavares walked over and gave them each a St. Christopher's coin. For luck on their travels. She did it every year.

"Thanks, Ma."

"Say the Hail Mary and be careful, Luciano." She kissed both her hands and pressed them onto Luca's cheeks, then hurried back to stand beside Mom.

Juni knew she was on borrowed time. Even though Anya thought she could talk Mom and Dad into letting her finish the trip, Juni was doubtful. But what would she do when the phone call came? Would she hang up and keep going? Or turn around and come home?

Juni didn't know.

"And we're off!" Luca said. Gravel popped under the wheels, and they all waved out the windows. He drove down their tree-lined street and out onto Highway 36. They passed the Holiday Market, the Burger Depot and True Value Hardware. And just as they were about to turn left onto Highway 89, a small group of dusty PCT hikers came around a bend in the road.

Luca pulled onto the shoulder. He got out and zoomed around to the back of the station wagon.

"What are you doing?" Gabby said, turning around in her seat.

"Giving away a little trail magic."

As the hikers approached, Luca gestured for them

to come over and handed out tamales. They barely got out thank-yous before inhaling those tamales like they hadn't eaten a proper meal in days. Which they probably hadn't.

Chester, California, was the unofficial halfway point of the Pacific Crest Trail, and all through the summer months, hikers would come down off the trail to pick up supplies. People in town offered washing machines and showers, and Dr. Lansford, the local dentist, even did free dental work in case of emergencies. PCT hikers were part of Juni's summer just as much as swimming in the lake.

After a few minutes, the hikers went on their way toward town, waving, and Luca got back in the station wagon. "Nine down, sixty-six to go."

He smiled. A big, toothy smile that Juni hadn't seen in a long time—thirty-eight days, to be exact. It crinkled his eyes, even, and Juni wondered if he was thinking about Connor. That if Connor were here, he would have smacked him on the back and said, *Nicely done.*

"I made a reservation at Convict Lake in Mammoth," Luca said. "We can drive straight through to the Wilders' today or we can take our time, Juni. Maybe camp tonight and head over there first thing. This might be my last trip for a while, and I'd like to stretch it out with you bozos."

"Nope. We have to stick to a schedule," Juni said, thinking how Dad or Mom could call at any minute. "Anya told me she knew where we were going."

Mason and Gabby gasped, and then Gabby smacked Luca on the shoulder. "How could you?"

"I had to tell at least one of them," Luca said. "I figured Anya was the only one who probably wouldn't say no."

"Probably!" Gabby said.

Juni kicked herself again for thinking she could trust Luca.

Gabby put a hand over her heart. "Honestly, though? I thought I might die from the stress of keeping a secret this big."

"You can't die from keeping a secret," Mason said.

"Of course you can. Oh, gosh! Is she going to tell our parents?"

"Anya said it wasn't right to keep it from them," Juni said. "But she's giving us a head start and hopes she can talk them into it."

"We'll be grounded forever," Mason said. "They won't let us see any concerts or get a job or go to college or get married or anything. It will be epic."

"At least we'll be grounded together. Do you think they'll take away club soccer?" Gabby did not sound as upset by the idea as Juni would have thought.

They drove in silence for a few miles until Luca said, "I'm assuming you have a plan for what to say to the Wilders?"

"I'm just going to tell them that we need Elsie more than they do." It was the only argument Juni thought she would need.

"We should look for them on Facebook!" Mason said. "Old people are always on Facebook!"

"Here, use my phone. I'm already signed in," Luca said. "And I'm not old."

"Pfft," Juni said. "You act like it."

Mason touched the screen of Luca's phone. "There are a lot of John Wilders."

He finally found one that looked right. The profile showed he was retired U.S. Army and worked for a company in Mammoth Lakes.

"His profile is private, so we can't see anything else. Luca, do you mind if we friend him?"

"How do you know all this? You aren't allowed on Facebook, either," Gabby said.

Mason gave her a look. Because Mason knew stuff. Not necessarily important facts, the kind you'd find on a test. But he could tell you a million little interesting things he'd discovered while searching the internet for test facts. Like how Facebook works or how to use a loom or work a combine tractor or shoe a horse. He was obsessed with yurts at the moment and was attempting to build one in the back corner of their yard next to the pet cemetery, which Gabby insisted was creepy and therefore, wouldn't help.

Mr. and Mrs. Wheeler encouraged him to follow his passions, which changed every time he discovered something new and interesting.

"Go ahead," Luca said.

"Here, you do it," Mason said, handing the phone to Juni.

Juni hesitated, feeling the enormity of it all. Her missing brother. The Grimm family curse. The quest that would help her break it. It was like a boulder going downhill. She couldn't stop it now even if she wanted to.

Juni poked the button.

Just then, Luca pushed an 8-track tape into the Caprice's stereo system. The previous owner had left a box of them in the back, and Connor had played them all the time. When Juni was especially missing him, she'd play them, too—Johnny Cash or Loretta Lynn—listening to them sing about walking the line or hearing the train a-comin' or being a coal miner's daughter.

Luca had chosen "King of the Road" by Roger Miller.

Which was such a Luca thing to do. It was completely unoriginal.

"I hope you can forgive me for telling Anya, Juni." Luca reached his hand over the bench seat.

She didn't take it. "Maybe someday," she said.

VOX CLAMANTIS IN DESERTO

THIRTY-SEVEN MINUTES into their trip, and Juni was a ball of worry. Would Anya wait the whole two hours to tell Mom and Dad? Or less? They still had another half hour before they'd reach Quincy and Madame Ophelia's Crystal Emporium, so Juni only had a half hour to figure out how to explain this peculiar stop to her friends.

If Mom or Dad didn't call first and demand they turn around.

"Luca, I need you to stop in Quincy," Juni said.

"What for?"

"Um . . . Anya. For Anya. She asked me to bring her a very specific . . . creativity crystal. It's supposed to help her get through the last part of this book she's been writing."

Juni had exactly twenty-seven dollars and fifteen cents in her backpack and no idea how much a crystal would cost. She also had no idea how she'd explain her interest in witches and other curse-related information once she got to Madame Ophelia's, but she was certain she'd come up with the perfect excuse. Because of course she would.

She clung tightly to the antler bone and the shimmering feeling that came with it.

"I thought we were in a hurry," Luca said.

Juni glared at him in the rearview mirror.

"Okay! Okay. It's your trip."

Juni needed to clear her mind and thought now was a good time to dig into Anya's story. Or draw a fresh set of antlers. The urge to draw them had been building, the way it did each day, like an itch deep inside where she couldn't reach to scratch.

"What did you mean earlier when you said it's your last trip, Luca?" Mason said, cutting off Juni's thoughts.

Gabby, who had been gazing out the window, nibbling on the edge of her thumbnail, said, "Luca will be an EMT by next summer. He'll have a full-time job and won't have time for kid stuff. We won't either. We'll be getting ready for high school."

"It isn't the Olympics, Gabby," Mason said. "It's high

school. You don't have to prepare for high school. You just show up and do stuff."

"You have no idea how hard it's going to be, Mason Harold Wheeler the Fourth. First, there are the extra-curriculars you have to take if you want to get into a good college. There are AP classes and tutors and test prepa-ration. Oh, and volunteering! You want colleges to know you aren't a robot."

"You won't even take a break in the summertime?" Juni said. "When will we ever see each other?"

"Of course you can't take a break! Your brain forgets what you've learned if you don't keep it working. All the French and algebra and Shakespearean sonnets will drain right out of your head."

"That's good. I hate algebra," Mason said.

"Sure, laugh all you want," Gabby said. "Your brain is leaking knowledge, and you don't even care."

"Shoot. I'll get the Caprice seats dirty with all my leaking knowledge."

"Har, har," Gabby said.

With her dad's encouragement, Gabby had cre-ated an entire bulletin board dedicated to images of Ivy League colleges and their Latin mottos, her favorite being Dartmouth's "Vox Clamantis in Deserto," which meant "a calling voice in the wilderness." She said it made her think of lighthouses, how if you were lost, a calling voice was a beacon. Gabby loved poetry, and Juni felt this was evidence that somewhere deep inside herself, Gabby must believe in magic, too. She just didn't know it yet.

"So, Anya gave me a sort-of project. She wants me to read her life story," Juni said. "She gave me a book—it's a story she wrote when she was a kid—and said I should read it with you guys."

"Really? Even Abuela doesn't know Anya's life story," Gabby said.

Luca turned off whoever was singing "Bluuuueee *vel*vet, whoa, whoa." Which sounded to Juni exactly like a calling voice in the wilderness.

She opened Anya's old leather book, and a letter addressed to her fell into her lap. Juni unfolded the letter and read it to herself.

> *Juni,*
>
> *I have never told this part of the story. Even to your grandpa Charlie. When you read through it, I hope you will understand why. Even after all these years, it's still hard for me to think about. But I really have come to understand we are only as cursed as we believe ourselves to be. The time always comes for us to take charge of our own destiny.*

All good journeys end by facing the truth, and perhaps
I've reached the end of this particular journey—the one
that started with an antler bone when I was eleven years
old—and can finally face mine.

I love you and send you luck on your own journey.

Love,
Anya

Juni tucked the letter away in her shorts pocket, took a deep breath, and began to read.

"'If there is one thing that stands out after all that has happened, it's something Mama whispered to me before she died . . .'"

WHERE THE STORY ENDS
Summer 1960

If there is one thing that stands out after all that has happened, it's something Mama whispered to me before she died.

"You have to know where you begin, Anya, and where the story ends."

At first I thought she was talking nonsense, the way she had so many times toward the end. But then she touched the empty place on her chest. The place where the antler bone necklace should have been.

I couldn't help it. I gasped. She'd known all along that I'd taken it.

I tried to explain why, to let her know there'd been a good reason. But she closed her eyes, her mouth dropping open, and I knew she'd be sleeping for a good long while.

She died two days later.

When Will died three months after that, I convinced myself the curse was alive and humming. Their deaths were my fault. Just as bad, I let

Will die without confessing my thievery. That was how deeply I carried my shame.

Teddy and Abigail have helped. Helped in ways they'll never know. But I suppose I should start from the beginning. Not with the antler bone necklace. That will take some time. But I can start with Teddy and Abigail Scott and Hickory's Miracle Café.

Teddy and Abigail came to pick me up at the social worker's office in South Lake Tahoe on July 31, 1960. They were taking me to their home in a place called Chester, up north on Lake Almanor. I'd never heard of Lake Almanor, but Teddy said I should feel right at home there, seeing as how it's a lake town and all. As though you can substitute one lake for another. I wondered if he felt the same way about family.

Abigail reminded me of a snowy egret with her long, dignified neck and skinny calves. She had a careful way of moving, too. Like she was nursing a wound. Or had sore joints. Teddy had more hair on his face, in the form of a thick mustache and beard, than he did on the entirety of his head. He talked with his hands and moved around a lot and didn't quite finish his sentences. I later learned this was how he acted when he was nervous. At the time all I could think was how they were truly an oddly matched couple and that I had no idea how I had come to be in their possession.

Teddy loaded my only bag into the bed of their sky-blue Chevy pickup, and Abigail offered me the window seat. "This way you have the open window. It's a three-hour drive."

Right, because I wanted scalding July heat blasting my face for the next three hours. I honored Mama's memory, however, by being more polite than usual. "Thank you, Mrs. Scott."

"Please, call me Abigail," she said.

But I wasn't ready for that kind of familiarity.

We buckled in, side by side by side, and as Teddy backed out of the parking space, he beeped his horn twice and waved out the window to the social worker, Mrs. Deakins, who may or may not have waved in response. I didn't look.

I was too busy drawing myself a map. I plugged in a starting point of Lake Tahoe Boulevard and then drew landmarks like the bowling alley and Freshies Market. I was going to write down every twist and turn so I could get myself back here if I needed to. No harm in having an escape plan.

If the curse had taught me anything, it was that I needed to be prepared.

Abigail turned on the radio, and I noticed she wore glittery light pink fingernail polish. Mama had never worn fingernail polish in all her life, because she considered it "fussy." She wouldn't have been able to keep still long enough for it to dry, anyway, since she was always so busy with her hands. Playing Scrabble. Knitting. Reading.

Right then I figured I knew something about Abigail Scott. She had chunks of time with nothing to do but stare off into space as her fingernails dried.

Teddy started humming under his breath with the radio, the theme song from *A Summer Place*, a movie Mama had seen three times last year.

"Melodrama at its finest" was what she'd said. Mama was a sucker for melodrama.

I think about that day a lot, my first day with Teddy and Abigail. How if they hadn't been such kind people, things might have ended up different. Instead of having our own future melodrama, I would have simply arrived at their house and eaten their vegetables and gone to school and done a proper amount of homework and chores and it would have been like checking things off a list. I would have behaved myself, of course, so I could stay in one place instead of hop all over the way Lucy Williams had. I'd met her in the halfway house, and she told me the world was filled with horrors. I told her I knew that to be true.

If they hadn't been so kind, I might never have thought to keep them safe from the curse, as terrible as that is to admit.

But then we got to Hickory's Miracle Café.

"Why are we stopping?" I said as Teddy turned off the engine.

It was two o'clock in the afternoon, and we'd only been driving an hour. I'd already eaten lunch, and I assumed they had, too.

"I noticed you were drawing a map," Teddy said.

I quickly closed the leather notebook Mr. Halloran had given me "for my thoughts and such." Nice Mr. Halloran who took us in temporarily when Mama was in the hospital.

"I like maps," I said.

"Looks that way, so I figured you had to see this one. I'll get your door."

I would come to learn that Teddy likes opening doors. For me. For Abigail. For anyone who might need a door opened for them. When I stepped from the truck, I turned to see the tail end of an airplane sticking out the backside of the café.

I looked at Abigail, skeptical. She smiled and offered her hand. I didn't take it.

"They have the best ice cream sundaes in the West," Teddy said in his best cowboy voice. "And there's a story behind that airplane."

I supposed an ice cream sundae never killed anyone, and I was always up for a good story, so we all walked together into the café, Abigail brushing at the wrinkles in her cotton skirt.

"See?" Teddy said, pointing to the largest topographical map I'd ever seen in my life.

From floor to a very high ceiling, it was a map of California, its mountain ranges raised in peaks and painted green, the snowcaps white. There were actual sand beaches and even tiny redwoods dotting the forest above the Golden Gate Bridge and in Yosemite. Sacramento had a tiny capital building, and a California condor sat in a tree in Big Sur.

"That really is something," I said.

A man named Hickory settled us into our

table underneath the watchful eyes of a taxidermy buffalo head, and gave us sundae menus. He had burns down the left side of his face and spoke with Teddy about fishing on Lake Almanor. They seemed to know each other.

Once he'd left, Teddy said, "Hickory is alive because of a miracle."

"I don't believe in miracles" was what I said, like a reflex. "So if this is a story about miracles, I don't want to hear it."

For his part, Teddy looked mortified, and I felt bad for snapping. He wasn't carrying around my tragic story at the front of his mind twenty-four hours a day the way I was. He didn't know I'd asked for a miracle for Daddy, Mama and Will more times than I could count.

Too little, too late is what I'd say to a miracle if it walked through the door just about then.

"I'm sorry, Anya. I wasn't thinking," he said, fidgeting with the hairs of his mustache.

No. You weren't, I wanted to say. But I held my tongue. At least it looked as though he meant what he said.

"What is your favorite subject in school?" Abigail asked. Although it was a terribly bland question, I figured it was as good a place to start as any.

"I like to read and write stories," I said.

"Oh, I love to read! I have bookshelves at home positively overflowing with all sorts of books. I'll take you down to Miss Betsy at the library first thing so we can get you a card."

I read over the menu, not feeling like eating all of a sudden. I wondered if I was pale, or tinted green, the way Will used to say I looked when I was sick to my stomach.

Abigail had known me for a whopping sixty-seven minutes, but she noticed. "We can come another time if you don't feel like eating."

The noise of people laughing and silverware tinkling and Patsy Cline singing from the jukebox "I go out walkin' . . . after midnight" was a weight on my chest.

Abigail pushed her chair away from the table and stood up. She smiled. "We've got nothing but time."

She would be wrong about that. At least at first.

We walked back out the way we'd come. Teddy stayed behind, probably to explain to Hickory about his poor, pathetic foster child. Abigail and I waited with the truck door open so the heat wouldn't kill us.

Teddy didn't take long, but before he started the truck, he handed me a small circle of wood. It had been cut from the middle of a wide branch, maybe four inches in diameter, rough bark around the outside edge. At the very center, a soldering iron had been used to draw a complex outline of a cedar tree. It was intricate and beautiful and stirred a deep feeling inside me. Like floating on calm water.

I must have been more tired and overwhelmed than I thought.

"The cedar is a symbol of strength," Teddy said. "We're all going to need a bit of that, now, aren't we?"

He turned the key in the ignition, and the engine roared to life. And just as he drove back onto the highway, there was a loud bang! The truck going all wobbly until he pulled over to the shoulder. Teddy got out and inspected the front end of the truck.

"Flat tire! Never fear! I will have us home in no time!" Teddy declared.

"This sort of thing happen often?" I asked Abigail as we stood in the shade off to the side.

"First flat tire we've had in years."

"No. I mean bad luck."

Abigail looked thoughtful. "There was a time where I would have answered yes. But not anymore." Abigail smiled. She had a lovely crinkly-eyed smile that made you want to smile, too.

But I knew better than to believe her.

I tucked the piece of cedar away in my bag. Teddy and Abigail were clearly loving and kind people. And they really wanted a child. I felt it coming off of them like the warm breeze off Lake Tahoe in August.

Right then I knew I had to leave. My being in danger of the curse was one thing, but there was no way I could put them in danger, too. Or anyone else for that matter.

Who knew how hard the Grimm family curse might strike next?

A PILGRIMAGE

JUNI STOPPED READING, and they sat, quiet. She knew Anya went to Tahoe every September by herself, had been going since long before Juni was born. She called it her Annual Pilgrimage to the Lake. When Juni was nine or so, she'd looked up the word *pilgrimage*—"to go on a journey to a sacred place as an act of devotion"—and asked her grandmother why she did this every year. Lake Almanor was literally in their own backyard and just as glorious as Tahoe.

Anya had told her it was a way of honoring her past.

The thick pines and cedars of Lassen National Forest had momentarily opened to rolling hills, brown and gold from the summer sun, cows grazing. Juni thought how Anya had driven this very road with Teddy and Abigail, only going in the opposite direction.

"No wonder she thought she was cursed," Mason said. "She blamed herself for her mom and brother dying. Do you know what happened to them? What about her dad?"

"Her dad died in a trucking accident, her mom from cancer a few months later. Will died from pneumonia." Juni knew this only because Dad had told her.

"So, how was it her fault?" Gabby said.

Juni shook her head, thinking about the way Anya had fit the curse to her own situation. How, in a different time, Juni would have argued that the curse couldn't possibly be true, no matter how much fairy-tale sense it seemed to make. Juni would have argued that Anya was just a kid and had suffered unimaginable loss, and unimaginable loss could make your mind funny.

But then you go and wake up with antlers sprouting from your head, and logic doesn't feel like the best argument for anything anymore.

You have to know where you begin and the story ends. Anya's words the night Juni found out Elsie had gone to the Wilder family. Knowing where Anya had gotten those words felt like completing a circle.

"I can't imagine losing your whole family like that," Luca said, tightening his grip on the steering wheel.

Juni refused to imagine losing a single piece of her family. Under any circumstances.

Mason wrapped his pinkie finger around hers. He knew what Juni needed just by looking at her face; a touch on her shoulder, a silly note in her locker, time alone. He said he was an expert in Juniper-Creedy-watching. As though she were a rare bird, or a sunrise.

They passed a sign announcing they'd entered QUINCY, POP. 1,728.

"Meadow Valley isn't far," Juni said. She handed Gabby the directions to Madame Ophelia's so she could call out the turns.

Juni closed Anya's book and held it against her chest, her heart thump-thumping beneath. She concentrated on Anya's bravery in facing the unthinkable, pulling that bravery deep inside herself so she might feel it, too.

MADAME OPHELIA'S CRYSTAL EMPORIUM

THE DIRECTIONS TOOK them off the highway onto Bucks Lake Road, which Juni took as a sign that she was on the right path. Two wide lanes quickly turned into a narrow two lanes without lines or a shoulder. Luca followed the winding road, eventually turning right onto Silver Creek Lane, the forest pressing in on both sides of the car, ancient and dim.

"Look at that," Mason said.

Juni looked out his window just in time to see a crooked old tree, half dead, with a rusty bicycle wedged in its branches.

"Stop the car!" Juni shouted.

Luca pulled over. "What is it?"

Juni got out and walked back to the dead tree. Gabby,

Mason and Luca followed. The tree had grown through the wheel spokes, its gnarled bark devouring the frame of the old bike.

"Can't you see them?" Juni said.

"See what?" Luca said.

"It's a perfect set of antlers," Mason said, in awe.

Juni reached for one of the dried-out branches, about an inch around. They had five shoots, each an exact mirror of the other. They reminded her of the antlers she'd drawn on her picture window, seemingly growing from the oak in their meadow.

A hot breeze blew pine needles across the forest floor. A crow cawed nearby.

"This is the part in the horror movie where the audience screams, 'Are you crazy? Go back!'" Gabby said.

"Like you've watched any horror movies," Luca said.

"Goosebumps movies count as horror movies. They are terrifying," Gabby said.

Which was a fact.

Mason made a special place for the antler branches in the back of the station wagon. He'd wrapped them carefully in the light blanket Connor kept for spontaneous picnics and looking at the stars.

When they drove back onto the road, Juni read the mailbox numbers until she saw the one she was looking for: 569 Silver Creek Lane. She didn't see houses, just woods in every direction. Luca turned left and drove slowly down the long gravel driveway.

"The picture on the internet didn't look like it was in the middle of nowhere," Juni said.

Finally, they rounded one last bend and an old house came into view, taller than it was wide, and painted in shades of purple. Luca turned the engine off, and they sat for a minute, staring. Juni's astonishment didn't come from the color of the house sitting square in its own meadow, nor was it because of the fairy-tale scenes in the stained-glass dormer windows—six swans in one, a hedge of thorns in another, Little Red Cap's cloak in a third. It was because they'd just driven up to an honest-to-goodness gingerbread house in the middle of the forest. With a witch inside.

Not actual gingerbread, although Juni had the urge to lick the siding to find out, but an old Victorian with gingerbread trim. Maybe there was even a child-sized oven in the kitchen, or stairs leading to a stone basement with a single spinning wheel, its spindle sharp and waiting.

"'Madame Ophelia's Crystal Emporium.'" Mason read the hand-painted sign hanging from the porch rafters as he got out of the car. "Tell me we didn't come all this way for a crystal you could have bought from Juke at the Holiday Market."

"Tourist crystals are different from real ones. The last one Anya bought from Juke's went . . . bad. But she also asked me to do a little research on curses and witches. For her latest book."

"Crystals don't go bad. They aren't cheese," Gabby said. She'd unraveled all the little braids she'd been weaving so her ponytail looked electrified.

"Thank you, Madame Gabriella," Mason said. "So far on this trip I've learned that summer gives you leaky brain syndrome and crystals aren't cheese."

"Awesome! Now you know even more random things," Gabby said.

"But they are extremely interesting random things," Mason said, and he waggled his eyebrows at Gabby. "I taught you how to French-braid, didn't I? That is a life skill. Unlike algebra."

"Whatever. I would have figured it out eventually."

For a moment, it felt like old times, and Juni smiled.

They walked between two pear trees and climbed the porch stairs as large brass wind chimes bonged softly in the light breeze. The only other sound was the tap-tap-tapping of a woodpecker in the distance. Before Juni could knock, the heavy door swung open. Standing before them, Juni assumed, was Madame Ophelia.

She could not have looked less like a Madame Ophelia.

There was no flowing robe or pointy hat or wild hair. She wasn't old or covered in witch warts or tie-dyed scarves. In fact, Madame Ophelia looked exactly like Juni's third-grade teacher, Ms. Baker. Tall, thin and a little stoop-shouldered, Madame Ophelia was young, not much older than Connor, and had long, straight dyed-gray hair. Not white gray, like Anya, but brown gray, like a sun-bleached fencepost. She wore ripped jeans and a Pat Benatar T-shirt.

"Um, hi?" Juni said.

"Hello yourself. What can I do for you?"

"We'd like to employ your . . . services?" Juni finished. "I need a crystal, and a few questions answered. Do you charge money for answering questions?"

"Depends on the questions. I'm Lena." She extended her hand for Juni to shake. "Madame Ophelia was my grandmother."

Lena hung on to Juni's hand for a moment longer than Juni thought was normal. Maybe it was a witch thing. "What type of crystal do you need?"

"One to help with creativity," Juni said.

Lena stepped back from the doorway. She smiled as Juni introduced herself, Mason, Gabby and Luca, and shook their hands as well. Luca suddenly looked gob-smacked, moon-eyed and somehow zombified all at once. It was extraordinary, and Juni wondered if Luca had just fallen in love. She hoped not. They didn't have time for that.

Juni followed Lena to the main room of the house, which had glass-front bookcases filled with crystals and jewelry. Placed throughout the rest of the room—on tables, hung on the walls and crowded on shelves—were all manner of curiosities: a perfect forest-green butterfly wing under a glass dome, a jeweled skull and willow baskets filled with dried flower petals. Heavy red drapes framed the windows.

Lena walked to a bookcase and opened the glass door. She handed Juni a blue orb the exact size and color of a robin's egg.

"This is the one you need. It's apatite. For a type of creativity to help clear confusion."

"It's not for me, though. It's for my grandmother. And I'm not confused."

"Hmm." Lena swung the door closed. She didn't take back the robin's egg. "It's better when the person is here, but . . . let's see. Do you have something that belongs to her? Or an object she might have touched?"

Juni thought of Anya's book, but found herself reaching for the antler bone instead. "She made this for me."

"Interesting," Lena said. "Do you mind if I hold it?"

Juni slipped it from around her neck. Lena took the bone in both hands and closed her eyes. Juni glanced over her shoulder to see what the rest were doing, suddenly nervous.

Mason looked as though he wanted to wrap up the whole room and take it with him. He was going from one object to the next, pulling Gabby along, pointing and whispering. Gabby was clearly trying not to touch anything or let anything touch her. Luca still appeared zombified as he absently flipped through a thick book on a marble pedestal.

When Juni turned back to Lena, her eyes were open. Without a word, Lena went to a different shelf in the bookcase and selected a green crystal, rough from the earth. Lena gave the antler bone back to Juni, along with the crystal. "It's called malachite. It helps with the grieving process and releasing the past. I'll give you some literature to go along with them so you can see what they do."

"How did you know . . . ?"

Lena smiled. "The bone has energy, but everyone is grieving something most of the time. My grandmother used to say grieving begins at birth with the first big loss of a warm, safe home. Learning to navigate grief is a life-long practice."

Lena talked to Juni as though she were an equal, as though of course Juni knew exactly what Lena was talking about. Which she did, sort of. What Juni didn't know was what to say in return. Lately Juni felt like she was a horse with blinders and on the other side of those blinders were the right words to describe what was happening inside her, why people did the mystifying things they did, how to make sense of monumental catastrophes, like death.

Juni used to talk to Connor about it. How she could never find the right words to describe the terror of not breathing, the sense of her body betraying her. Words were so tiny next to the enormity of death.

So Juni stopped searching and simply nodded. She read the price tags on the robin's egg and the crystal. "I only have twenty-seven dollars, so I'll just take the one for my grandma."

Lena took them both from Juni and walked toward a large claw-foot desk. "It's two for the price of one today. Come, sit. You said you had questions."

Juni was grateful for Lena's generosity as they sat on a green velvet sofa beneath a bay window. Beyond the window was a freshwater pond on which two black swans floated side by side. Juni took Connor's phone from her back pocket to check the time. They'd left the house an hour and a half earlier. Anya would be telling Mom and Dad at any moment.

"What sort of witch are you?" Juni said.

"I'm primarily a hedge witch, with a few other practices thrown in for good measure."

That was one Juni hadn't read about. "What is a hedge witch exactly?"

"We are healing witches. We walk the hedges between this world and the next."

Juni checked again on Mason, Gabby and Luca, who were still rummaging around, throwing the occasional glance her way. Luca studied a taxidermy bat in a shadow box on the wall.

"Do you cast magic spells?" Juni whispered. "Because I need a magic spell."

If Lena was alarmed by her question, she didn't show it. "Spell casting is serious. What do you need a spell for?"

Juni worried that even Lena might not believe her, or worse, decide she didn't want to interfere with a curse.

"I need help finding something that's been lost," Juni finally said.

"Do you want to tell me what it is?"

Juni glanced at her friends and then whispered, "My brother."

Lena closed her eyes and nodded once. "I can give you a spell to recite by the light of the moon. A ritual meant to call things back. You will need something of his. Something small and personal."

Juni had purposely left everything of Connor's behind, not wanting a single possession to be lost or broken. She'd left his nine letters to her stacked in her nightstand drawer. His room full of clothes and books and paintings. The college flags hanging on his wall: Stanford, UCLA, San Diego State. The childhood army men in a line on his windowsill.

"I have his cell phone."

Lena shook her head. "More personal. Like a necklace or good luck charm. Maybe a book."

"What about a watch?"

"Perfect."

Juni's heart sank. She should have been happy to have it, even if it was lost somewhere in the station wagon. But she'd wanted to leave the watch until Connor came home. She liked imagining him plugging in one of his 8-tracks and, while Ray Charles sang "Georgia on My Mind," turning to Juni and saying, "Hand me the socket wrench and let's find that watch."

It kept her going some days.

"You should know before you do this, Juniper, that not

everything is meant to be found," Lena said. "Not every secret is meant to be uncovered."

"I understand." She did not understand.

Lena opened a drawer in the claw-foot desk. She flipped through folders and gathered several sheets of paper. She placed a few items—herbs, maybe, a candle—along with the papers inside a brown paper bag and gave it to Juni.

"These instructions are meant as guidelines. Spells are like prayers. Everyone does them a little differently. One thing I've done when I've lost something is go to the trees and ask for help in calling it back. Trees are a community. They speak to each other, passing messages along."

Juni thought of Anya taking her sorrow to the trees. She thought of the juniper that had watched over her as she took her first breath. The way fairy-tale characters always found themselves in the woods, searching for lost things.

"We should get going," Juni said. "We still have a long way to go."

"I'll whisper to my own trees for you," Lena said.

Juni couldn't help it. She flung herself at Lena, who caught her, expertly, as though she'd been catching people all her life. She smelled like sage and candle wax.

"Thank you," Juni whispered.

On the way out, Juni saw Luca slip a Madame Ophelia business card into his pocket. He smiled at Lena. He smiled at Juni. He smiled at the bat on the wall.

Juni paid ten dollars for the crystals and the magic spell. Lena refused any more. She even threw in a small jar of pear jam from her trees and asked Juni to let her know how things turned out.

As Luca drove out the way they'd come, he turned right on Bucks Lake Road instead of left, which would have taken them back to Highway 89.

"Where are you going?" Juni said. "We don't have time for any more stops."

"The PCT crosses Bucks Lake Road a couple miles from here. I'm going to leave more tamales."

Juni wanted to argue—she wanted to go, go, go—but instead tried to find a tiny sliver of room in her heart for what Luca was doing. She knew it had to do with Connor, the same way she knew she had to go get Elsie, and besides, there was something fairy-tale-ish about leaving tamales along the PCT like a trail of bread crumbs.

As Luca set out the aluminum-foil-wrapped tamales on a large boulder in the shade with a sign that said "For PCT Hikers," Juni realized he had prepared for this more than she'd realized. Juni knew how much Connor and Luca had looked forward to the Domingo Springs trip each year. How much they loved sitting with the thru-hikers and listening to their stories. The first year Juni had gone with them, after she'd heard one hiker named Apple Pie talk about getting sick, being hit with hailstones and watching a lightning strike start a brush fire, she'd asked Connor, "What sort of person hikes for two thousand six hundred and fifty-nine miles after all that?" And Connor had answered, "A person who doesn't give up."

That was Connor. He didn't give up on anything or anyone. Neither would Juni.

When they drove back onto Highway 89, Juni hoped the rest of her journey would go as smoothly as this first stop. By tonight, if all went well, two of the tasks would be complete: the magic spell and retrieving Elsie. The sacrifice would be all that was left.

Completing her quest was within reach. *Too easy,* Juni worried.

Because fairy tales were never easy.

THE DONNER PARTY 2.0
(MINUS THE SNACKS)

MASON REACHED ACROSS the seat and twisted his pinkie through Juni's again. She noticed the freckles on his knees, how they looked like brown sugar crystals.

Juni wanted so desperately to tell him, to tell all of them, what she was really doing. She wanted to tell them the curse was real, and not just some dramatic story passed down through her family. She wanted to say she could feel Connor through the antler bone, like she'd tuned him in on a radio station. She wanted to know if Gabby had felt it, too.

Even though Juni was surrounded by her best friends, she felt alone.

They'd been on the road just past three hours now, and Luca had selected Perry Como to sing to them "Catch a

Falling Star." Which was only slightly better than "King of the Road." The Caprice didn't have air-conditioning, and when they came out of the shade of the woods, the hot air blasted against Juni's face through her open window. She thought of Anya on her journey that first day with Teddy and Abigail.

It was nearing twelve thirty, and they had made it as far as Truckee, home of Donner Memorial State Park and lake, named for the unfortunate Donner party. Juni was beginning to feel just as doomed as she waited for the phone to ring.

"You know, Donner Lake is haunted," Mason said.

"How could it not be haunted?" Gabby said. She grabbed juggling balls out of her backpack. Practicing dexterity was part of her athletic training. "They *ate* each other."

"Why does everyone only talk about that one thing?" Mason said.

"Because they *ate* each other," Gabby said again.

"Well, that's not the only thing that happened on their adventure," Mason said.

"Only Mason Harold Wheeler the Fourth would call what happened to the Donner party an 'adventure.'"

Juni had never understood how a bunch of bad planners who made a bunch of bad choices and ended up eating each other deserved to have a state park and a lake named after them.

They'd come to visit the Donner Memorial State Museum in the fourth grade and learned that Truckee was named for the Paiute chief who had helped settlers navigate the Sierra Pass into California. Tru-ki-zo had been his name. There must have been more men like him they could memorialize instead of cannibals.

"It does seem really weird," Juni said. "I mean, didn't a whole bunch of other people come through here and actually, I don't know, live?"

"A lot of people survived the Donner party. Forty-two people, to be exact, lived through four months in a nonstop blizzard," Mason said, "and for your information, Gabby, they didn't *all* eat each other. Almost half of them survived, which is pretty extraordinary, in my opinion. Considering they only had shoe leather and bark water to survive on."

"And each other," Gabby said.

Juni snorted.

Mason had been obsessed with the story since the field trip, and when they'd started studying the California Gold Rush in social studies and everyone was supposed to build a mining camp, Mason asked for special permission to do a diorama of the Donner party on the trail west. Mrs. Blankenship encouraged them to follow their interests, but she did draw the line at the bloody bodies Mason had carefully glued down. Bothered by Mrs. Blankenship's censoring of true history, Mason built a hollow boulder in the middle of his diorama and stuffed the bodies inside.

Connor's phone began to ring in Juni's back pocket.

They all went silent. Because this was it, of course. This was the moment Juni had known was coming since they'd left three hours earlier.

She slid the phone from her pocket and tapped the screen. Mason and Gabby sat frozen in their seats.

"Hi, Dad," Juni said. She felt strangely calm.

"Juniper," he said. She could always tell his mood by the way he said her name. It wasn't going to be good. "Do you have any idea what this is doing to your mother? Any idea?"

He'd shouted the words *any idea*.

"Do you have any idea what this is doing to me?" Juni said. At least she didn't shout.

There were a few seconds of silence on the other end.

"You will stop this instant and tell me where you are. I'm coming to get you," Dad finally said, less shouty. The phone's tracking app must not be working in the mountains.

"We're almost to South Lake Tahoe," Juni said. Luca met her eyes in the rearview mirror, and she shrugged. It was sort of true.

Mason whispered, "Don't make it worse."

"How can it get any worse?" Juni whispered back.

"Put Luca on the phone," Dad said.

At that moment, Luca's phone rang in his lap. He pulled over onto a wide shoulder beside the trees.

"Uh-oh," Gabby said. "We're in big trouble."

Luca answered his phone and climbed out. He walked along the shoulder in front of the car, his free hand running back and forth along the top of his short hair.

"I can't. He just pulled over and took a call outside."

There was swearing on the other end.

"I want to talk to Anya," Juni said.

"You are not in a position to make demands right now!" Juni heard voices in the background. Mom and Anya. Possibly the other parents.

Juni considered hanging up on her father and wondered if this was what it felt like to be a teenager. Like for once you didn't care what your parents wanted because what you wanted was the most important thing on earth—in the universe, even. It was uncomfortable, scary, but also exciting. Which felt all wrong, like wearing someone else's shoes.

"Can I please talk to Anya?" Juni tried again.

A few moments passed.

"Juni," Anya said.

"They can't." Juni's lungs began to swarm.

Think about the bee smoker, Juni. The way it quiets the bees.

"I'm coming, too," Anya said. "Don't lose hope, my girl. Meet us at the Stag's Head Bookstore in Tahoe."

"You are not coming," Dad said away from the phone. Into the phone he said, "I'll be there in three hours."

He hung up.

"But we're not in South Lake Tahoe!" Mason said. "Why did you tell them we were?"

"South Lake Tahoe is a little past halfway between home and Mammoth. Maybe if we're closer to Mammoth, I can talk Dad into going the rest of the way."

Luca got back into the car, the driver's seat springs squeaking as he sat. "Well, the score is four to three," he said.

"What do you mean?" Juni said.

"Mom, Anya and Mr. and Mrs. Wheeler think we should keep going."

"Oh my gosh! Mom and Dad never disagree on anything," Gabby said. "Go, Mom!"

Luca went on. "Your mom and dad and our dad are 'very disappointed in our choices.'"

"So we keep going. Four to three means we win!" Mason said.

"Nope. They decided unless they all agreed, we had to go home."

A car whooshed past now and then, making the Caprice shudder.

"It's a little over an hour to South Lake Tahoe. By the time we get there, we'll have a plan," Juni said.

Luca turned around to look at her. "I'll take you to the end, Juni. No matter what."

Mason took Juni's hand and held it tight. "I'll be with you until the end, too."

They each looked at Gabby.

"This isn't a disaster movie, guys. Jeez," Gabby said.

Luca switched on the turn signal and drove onto the highway. "For Connor!" he shouted.

"For Connor!" the rest of them shouted together.

And suddenly, Juni wasn't as angry at Luca anymore. She felt the weight of it lessen, draining away, like water from a bathtub.

THE INFINITE MONKEY THEOREM

AS THE SUMMER-DRY pines closed in on the highway and then opened into fields of honey-colored grass, Juni's thoughts about her quest took a similar path. The idea that this was wishful thinking—a dream pressing in, keeping her from seeing the truth—would give way to hope and the wide-open fields of possibility.

Mr. Wilcox, Juni's pre-algebra teacher from last year, had once told the class about the infinite monkey theorem. How a bunch of monkeys hitting typewriter keys at random for infinity would almost surely, eventually, type an actual story. Like *My Life as an Ice Cream Sandwich*, or *The One and Only Ivan*. When everyone laughed, he said the trick was in the term *almost surely*. Because really, the probability that all the monkeys in all the world for all of time would type *Captain Underpants* was so tiny, the chance of it happening was next to impossible.

But technically, not zero.

So technically, even though Juni had absolutely no proof she could break the Grimm family curse, that didn't mean she shouldn't try. Even Mr. Wilcox would tell her that although the probability of breaking the curse was extremely low, it was not zero. It was *almost surely* possible.

Bing!

"That's a Facebook notification," Luca said, pointing to Gabby's lap.

Gabby tapped the screen of Luca's phone a few times, then quickly turned around and gave it to Juni. "Captain Wilder accepted the Facebook request!"

"What do I do?"

"Click on his picture and it will open his profile. You should be able to scroll down and see his posts and pictures," Mason said.

Captain Wilder had an American flag as his background image, and the profile picture was of his family, Juni assumed. Three smiling daughters and a wife.

And there, in the very first photo Juni scrolled to, was Elsie, sitting on a blue blanket, her golden fur brushed and shining.

Juni held the phone to her chest and steadied herself.

The photo was one of three Captain Wilder had posted. In the second photo, Elsie looked across the smooth water of a lake from the bow of a boat, her long-ish hair blowing in the wind. The last photo showed Elsie posed with three girls near Juni's age: one younger, one older, and one who looked to be her age exactly. Each of them sat on a wide stretch of green, green grass and leaned into Elsie like she was the best thing ever.

And Elsie. The way she gazed at the oldest. As though she was her very best friend in all the world. The same way she'd looked at Connor.

Juni's heart broke a little bit, which surprised her. She thought it had already broken clean through and would stay in two pieces until Connor came home.

Those girls loved Elsie, and Elsie clearly loved them back.

Juni must have made a small sound because Mason took her hand, and Gabby turned around. She reached for Luca's phone.

"How about we read more from Anya's story?" Gabby said.

"In a couple of minutes," Juni said.

Charley Pride's "Did You Think to Pray" played on the stereo as they drove along a ridge overlooking a golden valley lit by the early-afternoon sun. Thickly forested mountains sat in the distance with their tippy-tops still capped in snow, and Juni was overcome with the need to draw antlers. She felt them twisting their way from deep inside, through her heart, and making her head thump where the antlers had come in. She knew this feeling wouldn't leave until she put them on paper.

Before Connor had gone missing, the nearest Juni had come to a compulsion was matching her socks to her T-shirts. Red T-shirt, red socks. Yellow T-shirt, yellow socks. No exceptions.

She remembered how Connor sometimes came to breakfast wearing socks that not only didn't match his shirt, but didn't match each other. He'd lift one pant leg, then the other, which sent Juni chasing after him, around the breakfast table and into the yard, where she'd tackle him, refusing to move until he agreed to change his socks.

Drawing the antlers helped. It helped with the sock-matching memory and so many others: Connor and Juni shoved into the old saddle Connor had fastened to their juniper tree, watching the sunrise on every birthday; Connor taking Juni's waffle right out of the toaster and running off, late for school; the way he'd encouraged her, when no one was looking, to guzzle milk straight from the container.

Those distant memories clogged her thoughts and her heart and her lungs until she felt she'd scream and burst and suffocate all at once. The antlers were the only way out.

Where is he where is he where is he?

Juni turned to a blank page at the back of Anya's book, the place she'd said Juni should write her own story, and used Mason and their intertwined pinkies as inspiration for a twisty pair of antlers, the left side different from the right in honor of Connor's mismatched socks. Every once in a while she glanced out the window, knowing Connor's beloved Pacific Crest Trail wasn't far.

Connor had said the people who thru-hiked the trail were on a quest, each of them having different reasons for giving up five months of their lives to walk through the highs and lows of deserts and mountains, to endure the grueling heat and snow, the blisters and starvation. Juni had often wondered what in the world must have happened for those people to up and walk off into the unknown that way. Now she understood and felt connected to each and every one of them.

She drew that connectedness into her antlers as best she could so she would always remember.

When Juni finished, she adjusted her seat belt, ready to read more of Anya's story. "Moon River" played in the background. Luca turned off the stereo.

" 'It took me a couple days to come up with a leaving plan . . .' "

WHERE THE STORY ENDS
Summer 1960

It took me a couple days to come up with a leaving plan. First, I had to make some money. Since it would take forever to save for a Greyhound ticket, I figured I'd stick out my thumb and offer gas money to the driver. I was an experienced hitchhiker, what with me and Will having to get back and forth to the hospital when Mama was sick. I knew to look for loaded pickup trucks and friendly-looking people. Will taught me to have a good story about why we were traveling alone, to keep a pocketknife handy, and, if I was ever in doubt, *run.*

Earning money and hitchhiking to Tahoe were the easy parts, though. The hard part was figuring out where to go once I got there. If I went to Mr. Halloran, he'd just bring me to Mrs. Deakins and we'd have to start all over again. The only option was living in the fishing shack Daddy used in the woods near the lake. It was deserted years ago and half falling down, but it would be a roof over my head. It would be tricky to feed myself and keep warm, but as far as bedding and cooking utensils went, I figured Teddy and Abigail wouldn't miss a piece of silverware here and there. Maybe a saucepan and a lid. I felt bad thieving. That's how this whole thing started with the curse. But I was desperate, and desperate times called for desperate measures. I had to be alone so the curse couldn't ruin anyone else.

I also made myself a promise. I wouldn't talk about my other life, much as I wanted to. The curse had wrapped itself tight around my family for months, and knew our stories as well as I did. I figured if I kept quiet, I wouldn't draw its attention. It could be anywhere. Floating on a breeze close by, maybe, tracking my scent.

A week after settling in, I asked Teddy how I could make a little spending money. I made up a story about liking sweets and saving for a sewing machine. As he scratched at his beard at lunch one afternoon, Abigail offered to pay me a penny for every weed I pulled out of her vegetable garden.

I pointed at her and shouted "Sold!" before thinking properly. Just the way Daddy used to shout at Mama when she offered him a pickle from the fridge. Or a cold can of soda. "Sold!"

he'd shout, and Mama would roll her eyes and smile.

Teddy and Abigail both jumped a little when I shouted, and stared at me like they didn't know who I was. Which, of course, they didn't. That was when the lonesomeness walloped me again good and hard. I had twelve years' worth of habits and inside jokes and words that meant something only to me now. I didn't realize how much keeping it to myself felt like shoving a lid down on something too big for its box.

I realized too late that I had broken my own rule about hiding from the curse, so I slapped both hands over my mouth and ran out the door.

I ran straight into the ricegrass meadow, sending little white bugs into orbit around my ankles, and turned right. I figured I'd run along the lake path until I wore out. But as I crossed into the neighbor's woodsy property, looking over my shoulder to make sure Teddy and Abigail weren't following me into the trees, I tripped over a boy sitting against a large stone and nearly fell into his lap.

Then I noticed it wasn't just a large stone. It was a headstone. In the middle of the woods.

"Shoot! You scared me!" the boy said, nearly dropping his book. "Are you okay?"

"How could you not have heard me coming?" I shouted.

I was on the small side, and stick thin from lack of eating, but I must have made a racket flying through the dead leaves, thumping the ground as I went. I bent over at the waist to catch my breath.

"I was reading. Everything sort of disappears when I read. Mom says it's an affliction."

He held a worn paperback of *The Call of the Wild*.

"Is it good?"

"It's my favorite. I've read it eight times. Mom says that's an affliction, too. My name's Mason. You must be Anya."

"I am." I wondered how much they'd told him. Then figured it didn't really matter since I wouldn't be here long. He stood up, brushing dirt from the seat of his shorts.

The headstone had a carving of a dog collar with a tag, and the name on the tag said Izzy. Underneath were years marking her birth and death: April 1, 1955 to June 13, 1960. Just a few weeks earlier.

"I'm sorry for your loss," I said.

"She was a good dog. She saved my life," Mason said. He brushed a clump of pine needles off the top of the headstone.

I recognized the look on his face from my own in the mirror each day. He didn't want to talk about it.

"Anya!" It was Abigail off in the distance. She sounded worried.

"I should go."

"I'll see you around," Mason said, and gave me a salute.

There are many points along this story that have made me stop and think about destiny. The stories Mama used to tell about the Grimm family curse made it seem as though some of us were doomed. The curse would find us, no matter how or where we tried to hide. But she'd also talked about the miracles in our family. The way the antler bone necklace was made of powerful luck and kept us safe. It didn't make sense to me how there could be room for both a curse and miracles, but I was only twelve years old, and figured I was years away from understanding such things.

Whether my story is one of destiny or one of my own making, I suppose I'll never really know for sure. But Mason was meant to be part of it, and for that, I am truly grateful.

I didn't see him again for about a week. In the meantime, the lost antler bone necklace haunted my sleep. Almost every night, I'd wake up in twisted sweaty sheets, not sure if I'd yelled out, until Abigail would come—frantic at first, calm after a few nights—and try to console me.

I'm not sure if it was Abigail who asked or Mason who took it upon himself, but he began to show up in the vegetable garden to help me pull weeds. I didn't see him doing the usual things boys do, like carrying on outside, throwing a ball or walking to the dime store in a group to pick up a taffy or a chocolate bar. He didn't even swim in the lake, which was right in his own backyard.

He kept to himself, reading. He liked to sit in trees. His favorite place in all the world was his very own room. It was round, like a turret in a castle, and sat at the tippy-top of the Wheelers' old house. It was filled with books and magic tricks and a piggy bank full of quarters.

It wasn't that I wanted to take his money. Just like I didn't want to take the Scotts' fork, spoon, butter knife and the cracked plate. I didn't want the old saucepan that had been shoved to the back of the cabinet with the lid missing its knob handle. I didn't want the dusty sleeping bag from the attic or the canvas rucksack I'd found that was much bigger than my little suitcase. I didn't want the cans of pork and beans or Spam or sealed packages of crackers.

I didn't want any of it, but at the time, I considered it my destiny.

My one solace was the cedar-tree carving Teddy had given me. I kept it tucked under my pillow and prayed for the strength to do what I had to do, resting in the calm-water solace it gave me. And because I wasn't deserving of that solace, I decided that when I left, I would take the little carving back to Hickory's Miracle Café. I had to remove every trace of myself so the curse would leave the Scotts in peace.

The last morning at the Scotts', before it all went wrong, Teddy had launched into a story, like he did every other morning before he left for his shift at the timber mill. Now, I wouldn't say he was the worst storyteller I'd ever heard, but he was up there, even though you'd never know by the way Abigail laughed. She also had this habit of taking hold of his arm and saying, "Oh, Teddy." Like he was the funniest, most special person on this earth.

Which was especially generous of her, because even though Teddy wasn't the very worst, most of his stories didn't have all the proper working parts, the way Daddy's did. His stories were just a bunch of beginnings.

"You'll never guess what George Kaplan did this time!" he said that morning. "He accidentally took his five-year-old son's lunch to work with him instead of his own! Isn't that funny?"

Abigail laughed. I did not.

Because I'd become a professional at keeping the lid on my own stories, I'm not sure what came over me that morning. Maybe it was because I'd been listening to twenty-seven days' worth of "You'll never guess whats!" Or because, with the help of Mason's quarters, I was nearing fifteen dollars in my Folger's can and was planning to leave any day. Whatever the reason, I finally burst.

"What was in the lunch?"

"What?"

"What was in George Kaplan's son's lunch?"

Teddy squinched one eye and rubbed his beard. "I do believe it was a peanut butter and jelly sandwich, a chocolate milk and a Ho Ho." He chuckled.

"See? That's what makes it funny. George Kaplan is huge, and a man of that size holding a silly little lunch pail and eating a PB&J, probably cut into triangles, with a chocolate milk to wash it all down is what makes the story funny.

"I don't mean to be insulting, Mr. Scott, but you might want to think about the middle the next time you tell a story."

And for reasons I will never understand, seeing as how I'd just insulted him, Teddy burst out laughing. He even smacked his hand down on the wobbly Formica table for emphasis.

I went on. "For example: my daddy? Well, he loved to read books. Any old book. Westerns. Science fiction. Romance. He wasn't picky. They were as much a part of him as his elbows or the hair on his head. He always had a paperback squished into the back pocket of his pants, and this one time, when he'd been walking on a log down by the lake, he tripped and fell backward, straight onto a sharp nail. He waddled all the way home just so he could show everyone how *Animal*

Farm had saved him from a rusty nail right in the behind . . ."

Teddy and Abigail smiled in that sad way people had when they looked at me, and while I was trying to fight off the mist in my eyes, Abigail got up to do the breakfast dishes. As she took my plate, she put her hand on my arm and said, "Oh, Anya," as though I was the funniest, most special person on this earth.

A flash of lightning lit up the kitchen. About thirty seconds later, thunder rumbled in the distance, and I knew I had to get out of there soon. The longer I stayed, the more I put the Scotts in danger. So, after Teddy left for work, and Abigail went to her sewing room to hem a new dress, I went outside to take an inventory of what I had in my rucksack.

I'd kept it hidden in the stone gardening shed. There was a perfect spot under a small table piled with clay pots and a bag of mulch. I dragged it from under the table and unzipped the canvas bag.

As I was counting my change, thunder rumbled again and the light from the doorway dimmed.

"What are you doing?"

I turned. It was Mason watching me count his

quarters. He looked at everything else I'd set on the shed floor. The silverware and the cracked dish and the pot and the food. The sleeping bag and wool sweater I'd taken from Teddy's closet that very morning.

"Nothing. Just helping Abigail get rid of some old stuff."

Mason crossed his arms.

"I know you took my money," he said. "I'm thinking you must have a good reason for it, though, and I'll need to hear what that reason is before I decide what to do."

For all the storytelling that lived in my bones, I couldn't think of a single word to explain what I was doing sitting on the dirt floor of a gardening shed with a pile of stuff that didn't belong to me. The truth was all I had left.

"I have to run away," I told him. "I have to. Or the Scotts might be in danger."

Mason frowned. He sat just inside the shed door. "What did you do to put them in danger?"

"I didn't *do* anything. It just so happens that my family is cursed, Mason, and it's all my fault."

As though proving that point, the sky let loose a lightning bolt, which struck a pine beside the

Scotts' house, breaking off a limb. That broken limb fell straight down into the sewing room roof with a crack and boom.

That's when I knew I'd run out of time. The curse was upon me, and I had to leave right then and there, whether I was ready or not.

TRAIL MAGIC

"THAT IS THE worst story I've ever heard!" Gabby said. "Why did Anya want us to read it now, anyway? We need to be thinking happy thoughts. Positive thoughts. We're on our way to get Elsie! That's a good thing!"

Then she burst into tears.

Luca pulled into a small asphalt parking lot, bright white lines marking the spaces, and turned the car to face a pasture on the other side of the highway. He set a hand on Gabby's shoulder while she struggled to get herself under control. Juni looked past them to a black-and-white cow standing at a split-rail fence, chewing grass.

"I miss him, too," Gabby whispered.

It was unbearable, and Juni suddenly wanted to go home. Fear, swift and sure, wrapped cold fingers around her heart and squeezed.

"Anya wouldn't have given it to us without a good reason," Juni said, leaning her head against the window, even if she didn't know what that reason might be. Maybe Anya was encouraging her to be brave. Or simply sharing her whole heart, all the little secrets she'd kept hidden for so long.

Maybe it was meant to show Juni that loving a Wheeler was in her very blood, passed down to her like eye color and the texture of her wiry hair.

Little bursts of sadness was about all Juni could take. She knew how Anya's story ended, not in miracles, but in real life. And Juni's worst fear was how her own story, how Connor's, might end.

Doubt moved through Juni like a swift river current.

"I wish I'd known my grandpa," Mason said. "I don't remember anything about him except the smell of pipe tobacco. Sometimes, I swear I can smell it in the turret room."

"I think now is a good time to stop for a minute and eat some lunch," Luca said. He pushed open the car door, which gave a small squeak, and got out. But he didn't walk around to the back. He just stood there, perfectly still.

Mason leaned out his open window. "What is it?"

"You guys have to see this."

Juni gasped as she climbed out of the station wagon, not because her breathing had gone wonky again, but because an airplane had crash-landed into the back of the building's roof, the tail end sticking straight up into the endless blue sky.

It was Hickory's Miracle Café. Right out of Anya's story.

HICKORY'S MIRACLE CAFÉ

THE FOUR OF them stood side by side by side by side, staring at the airplane in the roof. Juni wasn't the only one with her mouth hanging slightly open.

A short man in a red San Francisco 49ers cap turned ribs on an oil-drum-sized barbecue under a pop-up tent. A handmade sign propped against a chair announced BBQ RIB THURSDAYS 11–2. There were five or so folding tables under the trees where several people enjoyed their ribs, what looked like potato salad and baked beans on paper plates.

"Mmm, smell that barbecue," Mason said, apparently losing his mind momentarily.

"With cow farts ruining the atmosphere, it's mystifying to me how you can still eat red meat. Not only is it contributing to the global warming crisis, but it's terrible for your intestinal tract," Gabby said, rubbing her eyes. "You should be worried for your future colon, Mason Harold Wheeler the Fourth."

"I am worried for the future of my colon," Mason said, licking his lips. "No lie."

"We've got to go inside," Juni said, pulling the sleeve of Mason's alien shirt so he would follow her. Maybe there was a reason they'd found this place, a piece of her quest waiting inside.

Hickory's Miracle Café was a wide barn of a building, and after giving a salute to Barbecue Man, Luca opened the large knotty-pine door. Just inside to the left was the topographical map Great-Grandpa Teddy must have brought Anya to see.

Juni marveled over the tiny cows along I-5, which runs up the middle of the state, Half Dome in Yosemite, and the farmland in central California. She found Lake Almanor and Mammoth Lakes. There was even a thin yellow line from the border of Mexico to the border of Canada. The Pacific Crest Trail.

"Hello there! Four for lunch?"

An older woman stepped from behind a glass case filled with pies. She was maybe Anya's age and as tall as Luca, straight-up-and-down tall, like a mop handle, with fuzzy orange hair, gray at the roots. Her name tag said Winona.

They were an hour outside South Lake Tahoe, and still about two hours ahead of Dad. "We're kind of in a hurry," Juni said, but she had to see what was here.

"You can't leave without an ice cream sundae. That would be like visiting Fisherman's Wharf and not eating the clam chowder!" Winona proclaimed.

Winona sat them at a wooden farm table tucked under a window. She handed them menus and told them they had buffalo burgers on special, and then she hurried off to yell at the fry cook.

"Buffalo! These people are barbarians," Gabby said. "I bet they have tons of Neanderthal in their DNA."

Gabby had gotten a DNA kit for Christmas last year and was obsessed with Neanderthal DNA. She believed it explained people who ate red meat and hated algebra, as well as other questionable behavior and bad attitudes.

As they read over the menu, Juni imagined Anya here all those years ago. Was it a coincidence? Or was it destiny?

"Did you plan this? With Anya?" Juni said to Luca.

Luca put his hands up. "No! I swear. No plans."

Taxidermy animals hung from the wood-paneled

walls. The stuffed bison, elk and buffalo heads, Juni recognized, but there was a whole bunch of other animals she didn't. Rodent-like things with crazy eyes. A lynx, or an ocelot, maybe.

"Definitely Neanderthal," Gabby said. "Look at those poor defenseless animal heads!"

"They're vacuumed every other day," Winona said, having just walked over from seating another table. Her smile had a gap between her two front teeth wide enough to catch a watermelon seed. "I promise."

"Well, that's good to know," Gabby said.

"Dead animal heads are not up everyone's alley, but they've been here since the beginning, so they're part of the story. What can I get for you darlin's?"

"I think ice cream sundaes are called for. And french fries," Luca said, rubbing his hands together. "I'll take vanilla with dark chocolate fudge."

Juni expected Gabby to give a speech about ice cream and french fries not providing the correct nutrition for her soccer training.

"Perfect!" Gabby said.

After they'd ordered from what turned out to be a very fancy sundae menu with about a hundred toppings to choose from, Luca flipped through the selections on the tabletop jukebox, and Juni noticed a large plank of wood above the window beside their table. Someone had taken a soldering iron to it. The words burned into the wood read:

MIRACLE

An occurrence of wonder

Juni thought about her birth miracle, as well as the other family stories. Great-Uncle Clive surviving that ball lightning strike, and Juni's diviner great-great-grandmother. Even Mason had his miracle story about Izzy the German shepherd saving his grandfather's life.

Why did some people get miracles and others didn't?

And what, exactly, was the opposite of a miracle? An unlikely calamity? A disaster? A mystical catastrophe?

Eventually, Winona came back with their sundaes and french fries and told them to let her know "if you darlin's need more toppings or whatnot."

"Why is this place called Hickory's Miracle Café?" Juni asked.

"Not from around here, huh?" Winona said.

"We're from Chester," Gabby said.

"Up on Lake Almanor. Caught a kokanee trout on Lake Almanor last summer. She was three pounds."

Which was impressive. Lake Almanor was enormous, thirteen miles by six, and the kokanee lurked deep with the catfish, wise to the early-morning schemes of fishermen and their hooks. Pulling a kokanee from Almanor was luck at its finest. Maybe even a miracle. According to the definition burned into the wood above their heads, anyway.

"Kids mostly don't believe Hickory's story. When you don't find it on the internet anywhere, you think it must not have happened. Tell me why I should waste good time telling you a story you aren't going to believe."

Winona rested her hands on wide hips and Juni had the urge to sketch them, nails bitten, knobby knuckles, reddish skin. She wanted to turn them into antlers.

"Try us," Luca said. His smile was half charming, even to Juni.

"I can use all the unlikely stories I can get," Juni said.

Winona studied them for a moment.

"Theresa! You've got the floor. I'm on break!" A woman in a hairnet behind the pie counter raised a wet dishrag in response. "Scoot over, then."

Gabby gave up her spot beside Luca and crammed in with Juni and Mason on the bench seat.

"Dig in! I'll tell it while you're eating. Ice cream waits for no one." Winona grabbed a fry off the pile and used it as a pointer. "First off, Hickory wasn't his given name. You know anything about hickory wood?"

"It's real hard," Mason said. He had chosen rocky road with marshmallow fluff topping and had already managed to smear both on his T-shirt.

Winona stuffed the fry into her mouth and chewed. "That's right, but it's also as strong as it is hard, so they use it for tool handles, like axes and hammers. They used to make baseball bats from hickory. Anyway, the next thing you should know is that this is a story about how a grove of trees saved ol' Hickory's life."

"Trees? Saved his life?" Gabby blurted. Caramel sauce and whipped cream dripped over the side of her fountain glass.

"See? You've made up your mind before you've heard a word, a sad state of affairs for a person so young. This is exactly why I don't—"

"Please," Juni said. She nudged Gabby's foot.

Winona narrowed her eyes at Gabby, but went on. "So that was Hickory. He started out a hard man, who had lived a hard life. Lost a wife and a baby son in his early thirties. Buried their ashes together in a grove of cedar trees he'd planted for them at the north end of his property. He slept out there most nights, probably hoping the woods would take him, too."

Juni thought of her dad, and Anya even, how they'd taken to the woods with their sorrow. She remembered what Lena said about trees communicating with each other and wondered if it went beyond that. If trees had a way of calling to those lost in grief. If there might be a comforting language they spoke through their root systems, or in the movement of their leaves and branches.

"By the time Hickory was in his fifties, he'd built up twenty years' worth of a hardened heart. If you saw Hickory coming down the sidewalk, you crossed to the other side. He was a drinker, and picked fights in Mel's Bar on more than one occasion.

"But he wasn't all hard. He collected stray dogs. Mutts. He was a pilot. One of the first aerial fire-fighters. He worked with rescue operations and put out fires with his bright yellow Stearman, which he'd learned to fly during World War Two. A solitary job that suited him just fine."

"That's the plane on top of your restaurant," Mason said.

"It is indeed," Winona said. "Now you have the back-story. The real story starts in 1959 with a lightning fire a bit north of here. He worked day and night, Hickory did, and maybe that was why he missed something in the

Stearman's instrumentation that might have alerted him sooner."

Gabby took Juni's hand.

"He'd just filled the water tank, and was passing over his own property to get to the outside edges of the fire when his engine cut out. He thought he was a goner, of course, but said he was ready to join his wife and baby boy. What had he been doing the last twenty years, anyway, but biding his time, waiting for death to come for him, too?"

Gabby squeezed Juni's hand with both her own.

"His plane went down at forty-five degrees." Winona angled her hand in front of them. "When suddenly, he said, the world turned to slow motion and silence. He thought for certain he was in his last moments, when just in front of him, through the haze of forest fire smoke, stood his very own cedar grove. He said it looked to him as though all the branches of those trees were knitting themselves together in a sort of frenzied safety net, and where he should have plunged clean through and smashed to a fiery death, his plane slowed and slowed, gliding through the branches of those trees, dropping to the ground below. He bumped his head at some point, and he said that moments before he passed out, he saw his wife holding their infant son. 'Free yourself' was what she said.

"Of course, he took that to mean he should unharness himself, which he did, and dropped to the ground right beside his plane. He was burned, and he was broken, but he was alive."

By then, Gabby was squeezing Juni's hand tight enough to squish her bones together. Juni wiggled her fingers so Gabby would loosen her grip.

"Surviving took the hardness right out of Hickory. He was a new man. He retired from flying and opened this restaurant instead, finding a passion for cooking and sharing it with friends. He took the tail end of the Stearman and attached it to the roof of this building as an everyday reminder of his good fortune. He stopped drinking, and people didn't cross to the other side of the street anymore. He fell in love with a widow who had four kids, and he was good to them. He died happy."

"That is a great story," Mason said. "Why doesn't everyone know about this? It should be a book. Or a movie!"

Mason loved happy endings and forced Juni to watch old movies regularly. *Singin' in the Rain, An Affair to Remember, It's a Wonderful Life.* Mrs. Wheeler said Mason was a romantic and had an old soul, and Juni believed this was truer than true. Her feelings went whoosh-whoosh-

whooshing through her body, like a plane dropping and dropping through a grove of knitted tree branches.

"So now it's your turn," Winona said.

"Our turn for what?" Juni said.

"A story for a story."

They all stared at one another, probably thinking the same thing. If Connor had been there, he would have been the one to tell the story.

"You have the look of people on a mission," Winona said.

Luca nodded toward Juni. "We are on a mission. For her older brother. My best friend. We're going to Mammoth to . . . pick up his military service dog. She's with another family right now, and we hope they'll let us take her home."

"Oh, I'm so sorry. When did your brother pass?"

"He didn't!" Juni said. "He's missing. In Afghanistan."

Luca's hands were clasped in front of him. He studied them. Hard. Neither Gabby nor Mason met her eyes. It had been five weeks, and still her friends didn't know how to react when it came up like this.

"How terrible for you," Winona said. She reached out both hands for Juni to take, gave a quick squeeze. "I'll be right back."

She slid her tall self out of the booth and went through

the flip doors toward the kitchen. About a minute later, she came back with a shoebox.

Winona placed the box on the table and took off the lid. Inside were five circles of wood with the image of a cedar tree soldered into them. They were each about the size of a coaster.

Juni let out a small gasp. This had to be what Anya had written about in her story. The cedar tree Great-Grandpa Teddy had given her so she'd remember her visit to Hickory's Miracle Café.

"When the airplane crashed through the branches, Hickory collected them and chopped them into rings. For days on end, he took the fine end of a soldering iron and worked his magic into the wood. There are only these few left now, and when I see where one belongs, I give it away."

Winona smiled her watermelon-seed-catching smile.

"'An occurrence of wonder.'" Winona pointed to the sign. "I burned those words myself as a reminder. It's easy to miss the wondrous things, big and small, when life goes completely haywire."

Maybe it was the way her face had changed when she talked about Hickory, or her lively way of telling the story. "You were one of those kids, weren't you?" Juni said.

"Our lives turned around when Mom married Hickory. Same as his. Now you go on, and take that little piece of Hickory's miracle with you. Sounds like you could use it."

Juni wished she had the words to tell Winona just how much.

A NEW PERSPECTIVE

BEFORE JUNI LEFT Hickory's Miracle Café, she gave Winona a long, tight hug. The story had curled inside her the way Penelope used to curl into her lap, leaving her comforted and feeling less alone.

Hickory's story had given her something else, too. The idea that a story, no matter how fantastical, was meant to be shared, not buried like something shameful.

And if you couldn't tell your best friends your deepest-down stories, who could you tell?

Gabby and Mason stayed behind to use the restrooms while Luca followed Juni out the back door to look at the airplane tail in the roof. Finding this particular café when Juni had read about it in Anya's story felt like her very own occurrence of wonder.

Song sparrows serenaded them from the trees, and Juni took a deep breath, allowing their happy trilling to fill her up. Luca was quiet, both hands shoved in his pockets as he read the small bronze plaque on the wall beneath the airplane.

A MYTH TELLS YOU WHERE YOU ARE.
JOSEPH CAMPBELL

"What does that mean?" Juni said, running her finger along the raised letters.

"I think it means a story can make you think about your own life, but in a different way. Give you a new perspective." Luca walked off into the grassy yard and kicked at a rock. Juni noticed the buzz cut he'd had all summer had grown out the smallest bit.

Before this summer, Luca had always kept his hair longish, wispy-wavy. He'd been known for his hair, and Connor had teased him about the products he used, how Luca spent half an hour each morning to make it look like he'd been caught in a windstorm. *Why don't you skip all that and just hang your head out the car window? Boom. Done.* Connor used to say.

Juni had to admit Luca had amazing hair, that his square jaw and dark brown eyes were handsome. He'd always been thin from running, something Juni knew he did every single day, through rain, snow or dry summer heat. But Juni suddenly realized that Luca was even thinner than usual, his eyes sunken. His hair was short now, even though he'd never worn it that way before.

A buzz cut like the one Connor got the summer before he left for basic training.

Juni was struck with fear. Was Luca going to join the army, too? Why else would he have cut his hair so short?

Before she could ask, Gabby and Mason walked out the screen door and headed in her direction.

"That was a heck of a good story," Gabby said. There was a tiny spot of caramel on her chin, and Juni cleaned it away with her thumb. Gabby took Juni's hand and set her head on Juni's shoulder. Then Juni took Mason's hand so the three of them were linked as they looked up at the bright yellow plane.

Juni was going to tell them everything. What she'd found out from Anya about the Grimm family legend, what she believed about the curse, the quest, all of it. Maybe she'd even tell them about her antler vision on the day Connor went missing. There was nothing lonelier than keeping a secret, and Juni was tired of feeling lonely.

She would make Luca tell his secret, too. If he had one.

"So, you believed all that?" Luca said.

Gabby blinked at her brother. So did Mason. Juni hadn't seen that coming.

"What are you talking about? You mean, *you didn't?*" Gabby said, also surprising Juni.

"Come on, Gabby. There's no way a grove of *trees* knitted themselves into a *net* and caught an airplane," Luca said. "He couldn't possibly have crashed his plane and survived."

"You think because one small piece of the story might be a little exaggerated or strange, it means the whole thing isn't true?" Gabby said.

Juni hadn't realized how much she wanted everyone to believe Hickory's story. Because of course she did. If they didn't, how in the world would they ever believe hers?

"Are you calling Hickory and Winona liars?" Gabby said, as though she were defending close personal friends.

"I didn't say they were lying!" Luca said.

"Then what are you saying, *Luciano?*"

"I'm saying"—Luca kicked at another rock—"it's irresponsible! If the trees saved Hickory, anything can happen. That's what they want you to believe, and it's not right to give people false hope."

Gabby put a hand to her heart as though she were

protecting it from this attack of not-believing. As though she herself wasn't usually a skeptic of all things magical and strange.

"Hickory's story wasn't any weirder than the story Connor used to tell about the day Juni was born," Gabby said, slightly out of breath. "Was Connor lying, too?"

Luca was not a person to lose his cool. He was steady and reasonable and someone you could always count on to drive the speed limit and eat all his vegetables. So, when he growled deep in his throat, Juni didn't know what was happening.

He picked up the rock he'd been toeing with his shoe and threw it hard and fast into the woods, where it plonked against a tree. He picked up another. And another. After seven rocks, he stormed off around the side of the restaurant in the direction of the parking lot. The birds had gone silent.

Juni, Gabby and Mason stood still as trees, looking as stunned as they had when they'd driven into the parking lot a little less than an hour earlier.

Before they had a chance to recover, Luca came back. "If you want to stay ahead of your dad, Juni, we need to get on the road." Then he was gone again.

Gabby stormed off after him. "Luciano!"

Juni held on to Mason's hand. "You believe it, don't you?" she whispered.

She knew it shouldn't matter. Her own believing had to be enough.

"Yes. Yes I do," Mason said, which was nice to hear just the same.

WHAT'S GREEN AND HAS WHEELS?

LUCA DROVE TO the end of the parking lot and turned right onto Highway 89. Juni watched as he took several deep breaths and drove his usual turtle speed, calming himself. She had a vision of Dad's white Chevy pickup driving up behind them, wide front grille looming.

They'd been at the café for an hour, so Dad was still at least an hour behind them. If they were lucky, they'd make it to Tahoe before he did.

Juni was on a fairy-tale quest, however. So anything was possible.

Gabby practically pressed herself against the car door to get as far away from Luca as she could. Juni remembered being that annoyed with Connor when he'd leave the bathroom mirror covered in toothpaste spit, and stubbly shaving cream blobs on the counter. Every.

Single. Day. She would love to scream, "HANG UP YOUR DISGUSTING TOWEL!" one more time.

"What's green and has wheels?" Mason said. When no one said anything, he repeated, "What's green and has wheels?"

"What?" Gabby snapped.

"Grass. I lied about the wheels." He snorted. No one else made a sound. "Come on. It wasn't that bad."

"Why don't you read more of Anya's story," Luca said. "Take our minds off . . . stuff."

Juni met his eyes in the rearview mirror and wondered again about her army suspicions. If joining the army might be Luca's way of proving he was as brave as Connor. Something Juni often felt the need to do herself.

She didn't want to think about any of that, though. What she did want to think about was how Anya's story ended. Juni hoped there might be answers she could use for herself. So, she traced her finger along the lines of the flowers etched into the leather of the book, took a deep breath and began.

" 'Before I get to the end, I need to make my confession . . .' "

WHERE THE STORY ENDS
Summer 1960

Before I get to the end, I need to make my confession. I have to write down my thieving of the antler bone in detail or this story won't be complete.

All I can say in my defense is that a person does a lot of growing up between the ages of eleven and twelve years old. When I was eleven, I believed I saw something nobody else could see. Not Will, not nice Mr. Halloran or his daughter Alice, not even the doctors or nurses or even Mama herself.

I knew she was dying.

And even though it seemed she needed the luck more than anyone, I figured I knew better. It was so crystal clear at the time. If only I'd talked it through with Will first, or Mr. Halloran.

I didn't think twice, though. I just took that antler bone right off Mama's neck and never told a soul. Not even Will when he was looking everywhere for it, frantic that losing years of our family's luck meant the curse would work its magic and she would die. Even then, I didn't tell him I had it right there in my pocket.

I felt my logic was sound. If Will and I had the luck instead of Mama, maybe she would live. Because we needed her more than she needed herself.

It sounds crazy now, of course.

I put the antler bone in my pocket for safe-keeping and took good care of it right up until the stitching ripped through and it fell out. Maybe it ended up in some car we'd hitchhiked in to see Mama. Or in the woods around the house. Or the lake, or the hospital. Or. Or. Or.

Although I may be responsible for starting this curse again after it had been mostly quiet, I will take all the fairy-tale bad luck this world has to give me before I'd let anything bad happen to anyone else.

Once I saw Abigail was all right, just shaken, and Mason and I had fetched Anita, his mother, to come sit with her until Teddy could get there to figure out the damage to the roof, I hurried back to the shed with Mason as my shadow. It had started to rain.

"Please, Mason. You have to let me go. I'll find a way to pay you back once I get where I'm going."

I told him a quick version of my antler bone story, my only evidence of how I'd brought on the curse, as I repacked everything into the rucksack. I also told him if he tried to stop me, I'd just do it again. And again. As many times as I needed to. Mason didn't say anything as I slung the bag over my shoulder and rushed into the rain.

So there we were, me running into the rain and Mason following, probably not sure, exactly, what he should do. And because everyone else was rushing toward the Scotts' house—because a lightning bolt and a falling tree branch is what passes for drama around here—it was the perfect time to escape.

"Can I walk with you?" Mason said.

I told him he could do what he pleased. He didn't say a single word to me as we walked the one and a half miles into town. I figured I needed to get out on Highway 89 a ways before sticking out my thumb. Didn't want someone I'd met in the last month to pull over and drive me directly back to the Scotts'. And I'd met a fair number of people, the Scotts being as friendly as they were.

Eventually, Mason did insist I tell him exactly where I was going. He even got Hickory's Miracle Café out of me, because that was going to be my one stop along the way. I would have told Mason anything, said anything to convince him that what I was saying was true and that he needed to keep it to himself.

But I think about this part a lot. The part where I didn't hesitate about blabbing the whole thing to Mason. The curse, where I was going and everything in between. I mean, it was like I wanted to get caught.

As we stood on the shoulder, waiting for a car going in the right direction, Mason said, "You know, I came close to dying last month. Got my foot caught in a branch when I was swimming in the river."

Water had soaked my hair and was running down my face. I should have thought to grab a rain hat. Or an umbrella. Instead, all I had was a dumb sweatshirt without a hood. It wasn't that I was uninterested in Mason's story, but I was a little busy at the moment.

"Thought I was a goner. I'd been under for a bit and started to get loopy, thought I saw a water angel and everything. Then my dog jumped in right on top of me, which alerted my friends to where I was.

"Once Izzy jumped in, they all dived down

and worked those branches until my foot came free. Taking that first breath was the truest feeling of relief I have ever known. But then Izzy got pulled downstream in the rapids and was lost."

"I really am sorry about your dog," I said.

"Mom told me I had a trauma and that I wouldn't be the same. She said an experience like that changes a person. I told Mom I didn't feel changed, but I did feel like I was taking a break from myself. She said that was normal, but at some point, I had to come back. We decided we'd shoot for September."

My ears perked up. That was exactly how I'd been feeling. Like I'd left my true self behind somewhere, and maybe, while I was running from the curse, I might find myself again.

"I am truly sad I will not get to know you better, Mason. I think we would have been good friends," I said.

He stayed with me until a station wagon filled with kids picked me up on their way to Quincy. I gave them a sob story about a mama in the hospital and a daddy whose car had broken down. It was a good story, one that would get me as far as Hickory's Miracle Café.

And only that far. Because of course that

Mason Junior went right home and told everyone exactly where I was going.

I sat there in Hickory's Miracle Café, thinking I was halfway home, and then watched as Teddy walked in the door, frantic. So I just put my head down on the table and gave up.

Giving up should be harder than it is. It was so easy to lay my head down and feel my whole body unspool itself. I'd never felt so defeated in my entire life. Knowing no matter how I planned, no matter how hard I tried to go my own way, destiny would pull me back into its cursed grip. I felt like a rag doll. One that had been squeezed into a floppy mess.

But I couldn't give up, now could I? I would just have to come up with a better plan. One that I needed to keep entirely to myself this time.

"Oh, Anya" was what Teddy said when he reached me. Which brought back to mind Abigail and how she had made me feel special a few hours earlier by saying the very same thing.

"Is Abigail okay?"

"It was the darnedest thing. That tree limb falling like that. We were so lucky it didn't burst through the roof. Abigail was sitting just underneath."

Lucky? Well, that was a fantastically Teddy-like way to look at the situation.

"Let's get a move on," Teddy said. "We have a long drive ahead of us."

Before we left, I excused myself to the bathroom and looked for Hickory. He was dusting off a china cabinet near a sliding glass door that led out onto a patio.

"Here," I said, and gave him back his cedar carving.

He looked at the carving and then at me. "No one's ever given back a miracle before," he said with a smile, and I realized I never did hear Hickory's story.

"I don't believe in miracles" was what I said again, and walked to the parking lot where Teddy was waiting.

I have since heard Hickory's story, and from time to time I consider changing my mind. But that is a whole other story, I figure. Maybe I'll write that one next.

Teddy drove to the end of the parking lot, but instead of turning left onto Highway 89, he turned right.

Toward South Lake Tahoe.

Which was a shock, let me tell you. My only

thought was that he must be throwing in the towel and driving me to Mrs. Deakins'. Mason must have told him I was cursed, and that it was my fault that falling branch could have killed Abigail. And even though I was the one who wanted to go to Tahoe in the first place, I was real hurt. Because I'd figured him wrong. Teddy wasn't a kind and understanding person at all. He was unforgiving and punishing and thought it was okay to take a child back, like I was a jacket that didn't fit. And if I'd figured Teddy wrong, how could I ever trust myself to figure anyone right?

Teddy turned on the radio to a country-and-western station where they played Marty Robbins and the Carter Family.

"Did you know," Teddy said after a while, "that the Carter Family used to travel the Appalachian hollers collecting lyrics for their songs?"

Which sounded an awful lot like what the Grimms used to do, but I wasn't talking to Teddy at the moment. Eventually, Elvis came on and sang, "Are you lonesome tonight?" and I wanted to say, "Yes!" Gosh darn it, I was lonesome. Even though it wasn't night.

I didn't say a single word until Teddy pulled into the Happy Homestead Cemetery—where

Daddy, Mama and Will were buried—not the El Dorado County Social Services office.

For the second time in one day, I was out of words.

"Mason said this was where you were headed. He said you wanted to visit your family and that, frankly, he didn't understand why we hadn't brought you here ourselves before now."

When he explained himself after it was all over, Mason told me he figured that story would get me in less trouble. But sometimes I have wondered if he didn't just see right to the heart of things from the very beginning.

"How did you know where to find my family?"

"It was in the information we got from Mrs. Deakins. Abigail and I wanted to talk to you about your family, but we thought it best to follow your lead. We were wrong. We should have talked long before now."

We got out of the car and stood at the grave site. It was hot and clear, three hours away from the thunderstorm, and the air was thick with cicada buzzing in the oak trees. I didn't have flowers, so I gathered three stones and set them on top of the family grave marker. A cheap, unmarked headstone I swore I'd replace one day.

"There isn't anywhere you can go where I won't follow, Anya. I don't come by giving up naturally."

And what could I say to that? I believed him. I believed that he'd follow me wherever I went, and I was terrified. Terrified I'd lose them like I'd already lost everyone else.

All I had left was to tell him the truth. About Jacob and Wilhelm Grimm and how they messed it up for generations to come by going back on a deal with a witch. How the curse was following me now and we were all doomed.

"Don't you see, Mr. Scott? I'm cursed."

"Of course you believe you're cursed after what you've been through," he said. And no matter how many times I tried to explain that they were better off without me, that they should go and find some easier girl, he shook his head. "You are the girl for us."

That was what he said.

Whether I was cursed or not, he said, he'd take his chances.

I cried then. I couldn't help myself. Not just because I was failing to keep them safe, but because I finally realized how much I missed home. I'd been so fixated on weed pulling and my escape plans, I really hadn't had too much time to think about how everything was gone. I wanted to see our house again. To go to school one more day with Marianne and Cookie. I wanted to read in the corner at the Stag's Head Bookstore with Mr. Halloran smoking his pipe in his office. I wanted to find Mama's antler bone and bring back our luck.

After I pulled myself together, Teddy drove me to the Stag's Head, where I fell into Mr. Halloran's arms and cried all over again. His daughter Alice was there with her own baby, Petunia. Then it was Alice's turn to pull me into a hug while little Petunia pulled my hair and giggled, which made me feel a smidge better.

We talked for a long time, and Teddy and Mr. Halloran struck a deal. I could come and stay when I wanted, to visit my family, or the fishing shack, or Marianne and Cookie, but I had to accept that it wasn't my place to make decisions for Teddy and Abigail. They got to decide for themselves if they wanted to adopt a cursed child. They promised they wouldn't try to talk me out of what I believed, but I owed them the same courtesy.

And then we went home.

Home.

It felt a little bit like I'd failed. Because I couldn't do it. I couldn't leave them again. I really didn't want to run away and live in a shack by myself, hiding from the world. If the curse was meant to follow me around my whole life, I figured that would become plain soon enough and I'd decide what to do when the time came.

But it also felt like I was where I should be.

Abigail says there are no guarantees in life, that we are only as cursed as we believe ourselves to be. She says the time has come to take charge of our own destiny.

I hope she's right.

And I hope that someday, I will believe in miracles.

286.7 MILES

IT WAS QUIET in the car for a long time. The way it must have been that day when Teddy drove Anya to South Lake Tahoe.

"Wow," Mason finally said. "Did you know any of that?"

"No. It explains her Annual Pilgrimage to the Lake, though. I didn't realize she'd been going every year since she was twelve," Juni said, surprised at a sudden rush of anger. Not because Anya had kept her story from Juni for so long, kept herself from Juni, really, but because Anya had given up.

Juni had hoped Anya's story would give her answers about what she was supposed to do with her own. Instead, it seemed Anya was trying to tell Juni to quit.

But she wouldn't. Not ever.

Juni wasn't going to stop until she got to Elsie and performed Lena's magic spell for lost things. Not until she'd sacrificed the most important thing she could think to sacrifice even if she had no idea what that might be.

Not if her father demanded she come back home with him.

Not if the Wilders tried to keep Elsie for themselves.

Not if the Caprice broke down or her friends abandoned her or she had an asthma attack and they dragged her to the hospital.

Until that moment, Juni had felt wobbly on the inside. The way she felt when she couldn't breathe right.

Not anymore.

"I have something to tell you guys," Juni said, deciding once and for all to trust her friends with the whole story.

BY THE TIME Juni was finished telling Mason, Gabby and Luca about the quest she'd put herself on—the way the curse had struck her family again—they had arrived at the Stag's Head Bookstore in South Lake Tahoe. Dad's white Chevy was nowhere in sight.

It was two thirty in the afternoon as Luca drove the

Caprice into a parking space overlooking the crystal-blue lake. He turned off the engine, which made a ticking sound as it cooled. They watched boats zoom around in the distance.

"You really believe it, don't you?" Gabby said.

"I do," Juni said.

"Then so do I," Gabby said. She glared at her brother. "Because I believe in Juni."

Juni couldn't read Luca. He wasn't expressive like Connor. Never waggled his eyebrows or winked at her across the table or laughed out of control. He never danced like an idiot when he got good news, or sang off-key in the shower or the car. He wasn't the person you'd ask to tell a good ghost story or top off the oil in the boat engine or even bait a hook on your fishing pole. He hated slimy worms and pop music and sad movies and the smell of gasoline.

But, Juni realized, he was the person you could count on to drive you 286.7 miles on the most important adventure of your life.

Anya had once said Luca was the string holding Connor's kite, and Juni used to think that was a bad thing. To hold someone back, hold them down. But really, she supposed, the string was the reason the kite could fly.

"It's a lot to take in," Luca finally said.

"I don't need you to believe me," Juni said. "I wanted you to know so you can help if I need it. Can you do that?"

"Of course," Luca said.

"Just think. We wouldn't have met Lena if Juni hadn't gone there for one of the tasks," Mason said. "If you plan to call her, you'd better get used to unbelievable stories. She is a witch, after all."

That made Luca smile. "Man, there was something about her, wasn't there?"

"Um, duh," Mason said.

"While you two contemplate the amazing Lena, I'm starving," Gabby said. "If we still have tasks to accomplish, I need sustenance so my brain will function properly."

"And we need to figure out how we're going to talk Mr. Creedy into letting us get Elsie," Mason said.

Luca hit the button for the automatic window at the back of the station wagon. Juni got out and grabbed the small cooler with the sandwiches Mrs. Tavares had made for their lunch; the tamales were meant for dinner. Gabby unwrapped the aluminum foil and took giant bites. She had a ton of small braids in her hair, and it would take a long time to unwind them all. Juni got to work as Gabby leaned against the car. It gave Juni something to do with her hands while they waited.

That's when the real fight would begin.

FLOOR MATS AND DESTINY

THERE HAD BEEN a time when Juni knew just what to say to get what she needed from Dad. He had always been on her side when Mom got especially panicked about Juni's breathing and what activities she should or shouldn't do. He'd never treated Juni like she was fragile, and so she didn't feel that way most of the time.

But it was as though her dad had vanished with Connor and left an imposter in his place. One she didn't know how to talk to anymore.

"Your dad is so stubborn," Luca said, taking a bite of his own sandwich. He'd plopped down on a grassy strip between the parking lot and the lake. "Remember that time he patched a small hole in the fishing boat with that stuff he bought off the internet? Me and Connor told him it didn't look like it would hold, but he didn't listen. We laughed like crazy when he came back soaked from head to toe. He lost the boat, his fishing gear, the whole works. Good thing he knows how to swim."

"Reminding me that my dad is impossible isn't helping," Juni said. She wiped a trickle of sweat from her temple.

"We might as well talk about all the bad news," Mason said. "It's three fifteen. Who knows how long before your dad gets here. Even if you talk him right into it, we won't get to Mammoth until near dark."

Juni had an idea. "I need to find Connor's watch. Lena said I needed something small and personal for the spell."

Luca knew about Connor's watch. They'd all helped Connor try to find it. "Right now?" he said.

Juni nodded and opened the back gate of the wagon. Connor's banged-up metal toolbox sat wedged against the side panel. She heaved it out, setting it on the ground beside the driver's-side door.

"We need to take the car apart," she said.

"Um . . . what?" Luca said, scratching his head.

"Just the inside. The seats and stuff. If the car is in pieces in the parking lot, it will give me even more time to talk Dad into letting us go the rest of the way."

"Are you sure?" he said.

Juni reached into the toolbox and handed him a socket wrench as an answer.

They watched as Luca unbolted the driver's seat and set it on the asphalt. Juni wished she'd known this had been the last morning she'd have in the car with Connor's watch. That watch had kept her company and given her a place to think about Connor for the last five weeks. It had given her a reason to get out of bed every morning.

"I have no idea how to get the bench seat off," Luca said, peering into the back seat.

When Connor had restored the inside of the Caprice, Juni had been there every step of the way, so she climbed in and reached under the back seat on the driver's side, feeling for the lever she knew was there. When she found it, she pushed the lever and pulled up on the seat the way Connor had shown her. Luca helped lift it out.

The bees buzzed in Juni's chest. She took a puff from her inhaler before she got wheezy.

"Okay, Juni?" Luca said. She felt his hand on her shoulder.

"Okay," she said.

It didn't take long. The watch had just slipped into a small opening in the carpeting underneath the driver's-side seat. She pulled it out by the black fabric band.

Grandpa Charlie had given Connor the Timex on his sixteenth birthday. *A working person's watch* was what Grandpa Charlie had said, much easier and quicker to check than a cell phone. Juni remembered Grandpa Charlie showing Connor how to set the alarm, telling him he wouldn't have to depend on cell phone batteries anymore, either. A man with a watch was truly in charge of his own destiny.

They'd all laughed when he'd said it.

Just then, Dad pulled in beside the Caprice. He opened the door of the truck and stepped out, bald head shining in the sun.

"What in the world have you done now?" he said, taking in the various car parts on the asphalt.

Juni climbed out of the Caprice to face him, fastening the watch, which hung on her wrist like a bracelet.

"I'm taking charge of my own destiny," she said.

HANDSOME DAN

FACING HER DAD, it struck Juni how it wasn't the curse that had turned him into a bear. He'd always been bearlike, growling when he was bothered. Like when he couldn't get his plump fingers to fasten a hook and eye, or reach into a small space, he'd roar for Juni—*Jun-iiiii-perrrrr!*—and she would come running, giggling at how her giant dad could be set to growling by something as tiny as the screw holding his glasses together.

He was everything to Juni. The kindly king in the fairy tale. The one who was always on her side. Juni understood everything was about to change, one way or the other. If Dad forced her to get in the car, or the truck, and insisted on driving her home and away from

Elsie, he would really and truly have become someone she didn't know anymore.

Anya came around the back side of the truck, and Juni ran to her outstretched arms, working hard to be brave. She had to see this through. Had to find a way to make Dad understand.

Think about the bee smoker, Juni. The way it quiets the bees.

Soon enough, Dad pulled her from Anya's arms and took her into his own.

"I'm so sorry, Juni Bean," he whispered. "I hope you can forgive me."

He kissed her forehead and they rocked there for a minute, or maybe it was a day, or forever. Eventually, Dad leaned back. "Now. What in the world have you done here?"

Juni held up her wrist. "I found Connor's watch."

Unexpectedly, Dad laughed. He laughed and laughed as he took in the discarded seats in the parking lot. "I'll say you did."

IT TOOK A while to put the car back together, with Dad growling at the Caprice as he tried to bolt the seats in. Finally, Luca took over, so Dad growled at Luca.

In the meantime, Anya led Juni, Gabby and Mason

into the Stag's Head Bookstore. The store might have been a lakefront cottage once upon a time. It stood alone, tucked off the road and nestled in the woods beyond the parking lot.

A tinkling bell announced their arrival, and a young man came from behind the old cash register to greet them, a fluffy dog at his heels. "Anya! You're early this year! Grandma didn't mention you were coming."

The dog sniffed Juni's shoes and then seemed to smile at her, like Elsie had in the picture with Connor. She had one brown eye and one blue. Her name was Norman.

Anya walked over and gave the man one of her quick wring-out-the-sponge hugs. The man's eyes matched, both brown. He had a lumberjack beard. "Nathan. It's good to see you. Is Alice here?"

"Couldn't keep Grandma away, even if we tried," Nathan said. "Grandma!"

As they waited, Juni noticed a wall of pictures to their left. Family photos, and an old black-and-white of the Stag's Head with a man standing in the doorway, a big smile on his face and a beard the same as Nathan's. Juni wondered if that was the Mr. Halloran Anya had written about, Alice's father.

Anya put her arm around Juni and they looked at the old photos, Anya pointing to one of her as a small child, and one of Will. Teddy and Abigail. Juni's guess was correct as Anya pointed out Mr. Halloran. Juni stared extra long at Will, who looked so much like Connor—same wavy dark hair, same wide-set dark eyes. Anya's story came to life on the wall in front of them.

"This is where you come on your pilgrimage, right?" Juni said.

"I still wander the woods looking for the antler bone. I know it's long gone, but I look anyway. I visit my family. I go through old photographs and remember. Maybe it's time for something new."

"Anya, my love." A very old woman walked toward them, leaning on a wooden cane. Her hair was snow white and sparse, like flour spread thin on a cutting board.

"Alice," Anya said. She took Alice's hands and held tight.

"I was so sorry to hear about your grandson," Alice said. Her face had a thousand crinkly wrinkles. A million. "I recognize Juniper from her photographs, and who else do we have here?"

After introductions, Dad came in, with Luca following right behind.

"Handsome Dan!" Alice said, and shuffled toward Dad, who gave her a delicate hug. "What brings all of you to our neck of the woods earlier than usual this year?"

Every last person looked at Juni, who didn't hesitate. "We're going to bring home Connor's dog," she said.

"Let's make ourselves comfortable, then. It seems there is a story here, and I'd like to know what it is," Alice said.

Anya pushed a lock of hair behind Juni's ear. "It's your story now."

AN OCCURRENCE OF WONDER

IT WAS FOUR o'clock and too late to drive to Mammoth, so they decided to start first thing in the morning. No stopping for miracles this time, or ice cream sundaes or gingerbread houses in the woods. They would drive the 139 remaining miles straight through.

In the meantime, Alice invited them to stay overnight at her cabin. There was enough room for the adults inside, and the kids could assemble their tent and sleep beside the lake. They would have a great feast of tamales for dinner.

Alice wanted to make a stop first, though. For Anya.

Nathan closed the bookstore early and helped his grandmother into his Prius, then opened the back door for Norman to hop in. They drove out of the parking lot in a caravan, Nathan leading the way.

Luca had selected Patsy Cline out of Connor's box

of 8-track tapes, and as Patsy sang "I Fall to Pieces" and "Crazy," Juni took comfort in the confident sound of her voice. She sang stories about love and loss as though she'd actually fallen to pieces and gone crazy and lived to tell the tale. Patsy seemed to be saying that if she could do it, well, gosh darn it, so could you.

Soon enough, the Prius turned down a two-lane road and made a sharp left into a long driveway. Each car passed a low brick sign.

HAPPY HOMESTEAD CEMETERY

"This is where Anya's family is buried," Gabby said solemnly.

Juni closed her eyes, the hot breeze from Gabby's open window blowing the waves of her hair. *Hurricane hair* was what Connor used to call it.

After parking, Juni watched Anya climb down from the truck and look out over the pale headstones. The cemetery was in a small valley, flat and covered in what might have been the greenest grass Juni had ever seen, the majesty of Monument Peak in the distance. There were ponderosa and sugar pines here and there, but most of the grave sites were in the open with an unobstructed view of the sun and sky, the stars at night.

Anya started off toward the left side of the cemetery, and Juni followed. Everyone else stayed behind. Anya wore a sleeveless white blouse, short pants and her trusty hiking sandals. She wore them all summer because she liked to be prepared for when the urge to go walking came over her. The woods would call, she said, and she'd always come home with treasures: singular rocks or a perfectly symmetrical pinecone. An abandoned hummingbird nest the size of a walnut shell. Anya kept those treasures on shelves Grandpa Charlie had made special for that very purpose. There were bluebird eggshells and hunks of quartz and a basket she'd woven from pine needles, and Juni felt each piece was as much a part of Anya as her ancient blue eyes or the stories she told.

Anya finally stopped in front of a large headstone with three names carved into it.

Juni read the names of her family.

Emily Katherine Weisert
Hubbard Leon Weisert
William Hubbard Weisert

"Mama loved sauerkraut. She put it on everything. Tuna fish sandwiches. Hamburgers. Scrambled eggs. And Dad was a reader. He used to buy paperbacks from Friends of the Library for five cents apiece," Anya said. "Will liked practical jokes. He'd hide my favorite sweater, put a rubber snake under my pillow or turn the clock forward so I thought I was late for school."

A flock of dark-bellied geese honked overhead in the late-afternoon sunshine, flying toward a large pond in the distance. Juni shaded her eyes and watched them land one by one. *Splash. Splash. Splash.*

"Why didn't you ever tell anyone what happened?" Juni said.

"I didn't want anyone else to have to carry the burden, but there comes a time when stories need to be told. This was the right time for both of us, I think."

Anya reached into her pocket and took out three flat pebbles. There was a vase attached to the headstone near the bottom filled with similar pebbles, and Juni remembered the part of Anya's story where Teddy had driven her here for the first time. How she didn't have flowers, so she'd left pebbles instead. The headstone was beautiful.

"Mrs. Wheeler carved this," Juni said.

Anya nodded.

Juni rested against Anya's arm, considering how Anya had lost her whole world and managed, somehow, to go on. Which, Juni figured, was its own sort of miracle. She reached into her pocket for the carved cedar tree from Hickory's.

"I think you can have this back now."

Anya put a hand to her mouth in surprise. She took the carving from Juni and pressed it against her chest. "I think you're right."

THEY SET UP the large tent, each of them taking turns banging the metal pylons into the soft earth of Alice's yard, which ended at a sandy beach, the lake beyond. Anya would sleep in the guest room as, Juni found out, she'd been doing for the last fifty-eight years. Alice's little cottage was nestled in a sea of trees.

Eventually, the sun dipped past the mountains on the far side of the lake, leaving the sky a bright orange. They collected brushwood for kindling and sat in beach chairs as Nathan built a fire in a stone firepit.

"One dollar says the sunset will turn the sky pink." Gabby reached into her jean shorts pocket, pulled out a rumpled dollar bill and waved it around.

"I'm in. I say red," Dad said.

"I'm going with purple," Juni said.

Once they'd each chosen colors, they sat quietly and waited for the sky to decide.

Gabby won. So did Dad. And so did Juni, if you counted the clouds. The pink-red-purple sky turned the lake into a kaleidoscope, and a hush came over the world. As though the animals in the woods, the birds in the trees and even the wind itself were taking it all in.

Long after sunset—when the crackling fire had turned to embers, and the adults went inside for a glass of wine—

Juni gathered Mason, Gabby and Luca to perform Lena's magic spell. They walked a little ways into the woods, climbed over a fallen tree and sat in a circle, Juni setting a flashlight in the middle. The directions Lena had placed in the paper bag were simple. Juni was to set Connor's watch beside the flashlight, and they were each to hold him in their thoughts, imagining a cord connecting them, pulling Connor home.

Then they told stories.

Like the time Luca and Connor had taken Juni, Mason and Gabby snipe hunting in the woods when they'd been in the third grade. It was dark, and the boys had told the trio they were to stand under a pine tree, holding an open burlap sack. Connor told them to yodel, and then the snipes would run straight into the bag because they were very dumb and liked yodeling. Only, Juni had already heard from Mary Jo Bingly how snipes weren't real, but everyone's dumb big brother had to at least give it a try. She said it's what big brothers talked about in the locker room at school. Fake snipe hunting and chess strategies, all while flexing their biceps.

So they were prepared. Mason had recorded the roar of the Tyrannosaurus rex from the *Jurassic Park* movie on his phone and borrowed his mom's portable speaker for extra volume. Once they were in position near their chosen trees, Luca and Connor trying hard not to laugh too loud, Mason let the recording go at top volume.

Instead of running away like cowards, though, both Connor and Luca had run straight for Juni, Mason and Gabby, herding them through the woods like sheep. By the time they stomped up the deck stairs, Juni, Mason and Gabby were bent over laughing. Mason played the recording again, and Luca and Connor chased them until they all fell into a pile.

"Don't join the army," Juni said to Luca in the quiet of their circle. "Connor wouldn't want you to."

"What?" Gabby said.

"What are you talking about?" Luca said.

"Your hair. You cut it short. Just like Connor did last summer before he left for basic training," Juni said.

Luca touched his hair. "I'm not going to join the army, Juni. It's not about that."

They waited for Luca to say more, faces shadowed by the harsh flashlight.

"Connor gave me such a hard time, you know? About my hair. Every morning when I looked in the mirror, all I heard was Connor's voice, and I just didn't want to hear it for a while."

Which was not what Juni expected, but she understood perfectly.

They laughed about Connor's obsession with keeping his sneakers clean, and the many times he tried to grow a mustache, and all his failed attempts at learning to play guitar.

Eventually, they were quiet and Juni knew this part was finished. She fastened the watch to her wrist and led the way back to the firepit. She spoke to the trees as she went, hoping they'd pass the message along. *Find him and bring him home to me.*

When Anya used to take Connor and Juni on walks in the woods, she'd always talk to the cedars. She would tell the trees their own birth story, how the red-throated loon had carried the future in her mouth, winged seeds falling out and taking root. Anya told the trees she loved their loyalty in tending the stumps in their grove because, even though the trees themselves may have died, the roots were part of a system that didn't want to let them go. She said she could hear them breathe, knew their hearts, and because they were witness to love and rain, wind and anger, they held the story of Juniper's family, of time itself, deep in their graceful limbs.

Juni longed for the familiarity of her own woods, to walk with Connor again and listen to Anya talk to the trees.

Feeling as though she had lived through the longest day of her life, Juni decided to sleep under the stars instead of in the tent. She unrolled her sleeping bag on the soft wild grass and lay on it, hands behind her head. Mason and Gabby stretched their bags out on either side of Juni's and joined her to watch the sky for shooting stars. Eventually, Dad crunched along the gravel pathway, appeared above Juni and kneeled to kiss her forehead.

"I called the Wilders," he said. "They're looking forward to meeting us."

"You didn't tell them . . ."

"I didn't tell them why we were coming, no. I figured you'd want to do that for yourself."

Juni flipped to her stomach and propped herself up on her elbows so she could look at her dad properly. He was backlit from the porch lights, so she couldn't see his expression very well. The moonlight only gave her a wrinkled brow and a frown.

"What is it?" she said.

"We can still go back, Juni. These types of things never go the way we hope they will," Dad said.

"Now you sound like Mom."

"We can't have come all this way and not finish what we started, Mr. Creedy," Gabby said. "We aren't quitters."

"Knowing when to quit is as important as knowing when not to quit," Dad said. "It's an art, not a science."

"I'm going to need an example of when it's okay to quit," Gabby said.

"You wouldn't blame Juni for wanting to go home right now, right?" Mason said.

"Of course not!"

"There's your example."

Juni was certain Gabby's head had just exploded.

"Have you thought about what you're going to say to the Wilders?" Dad said. He'd picked up a pebble and rubbed it between his thumb and fingers.

"A little. But then I thought it should be spontaneous, from my heart. If I try to plan, it will be coming from my brain, which isn't so reliable when I'm nervous. Especially if my breathing goes funny."

Juni was specifically thinking of the speech she'd almost given last year on the importance of oral hygiene. Almost, because once she was standing in front of Mr. Humburger's class, she couldn't remember a single word of it. Not even the interesting fact Mason had discovered about how a mouth was dirtier than a toilet bowl.

"Well, then. They haven't got a chance," Dad said. He kissed Juni on the forehead again and left her to her thoughts.

Soon enough, Gabby was snoring—she could fall

asleep anywhere—leaving Juni and Mason to stare at the Milky Way alone, sort of. Juni glanced over at Mason and noticed the curve of his collarbone, the hollow at the center. She wondered if that hollow was deep enough to grow a shallow-rooted plant, like a succulent.

"Why do they call it the Milky Way?" Juni said. "Please don't tell me they named it after a candy bar."

Mason snorted. "It could be the ancient Romans are to blame. Or the Greeks. No one knows for sure. But around twenty-five hundred years ago, someone started calling it Via Lactea, which means 'Road of Milk,' because of the milky band of stars running through the middle. Not very original, I guess."

"Like mine. Juniper. I was named after a tree that happened to be there when I started breathing. What would they have named me if I had been next to a pine? I guess Aspen would have been cool."

"I like Poison Ivy," Mason said.

"Blackberry."

"Pinecone!"

They giggled together, both of them pulling the sleeping bags over their heads to muffle the sound. Gabby snorted in her sleep. She was probably drooling.

Once they'd quieted, Mason turned on his side to face Juni, so she turned on her side, too.

"Are you scared?" Mason said. "About tomorrow?"

"Not as much as I thought I'd be."

Because this was it. The end of her quest. She should have been terrified of what was to come, how she might fail. But it was hard to hang on to the scared feelings with the Milky Way above her, the ancient trees beyond carrying her magic spell away and away.

Juni almost didn't recognize her own hand as she ran two fingers along Mason's jawbone, ending at his chin. She touched the fine hairs he'd have to shave off one day, like Dad.

"Okay?" she said.

"Okay," he said.

Juni leaned forward and touched her lips to his. This went on for minutes, hours, days, and did not feel the way she'd thought it would—dizzying or strange. Those were small words, ordinary words. Pre-kiss words.

Instead, Juni felt a new galaxy form inside of her, as though she'd exploded into a trillion tiny particles of light.

BRAVE AND STRONG

CONNOR'S WATCH WOKE Juni at 6:35. She put her arm under her pillow to muffle the sound, and drifted back to sleep. There, she found a little shack in the woods, a girl sitting by the fire, petting the coarse fur of a young buck. Next thing Juni knew, Dad was beside her. "Time to get a move on."

Juni, Gabby and Mason each rolled their sleeping bags and got to work with Luca taking the tent apart while Dad stood at the water's edge. He drank coffee from a large misshapen blue mug, the same cerulean as the deep water of Lake Tahoe. Nathan and Anya were inside making breakfast, the smell of bacon floating in the morning breeze.

For the first time ever, Juni felt shy around Mason,

felt her face burn when he came close. She was sweaty and awkward and generally flustered in a way she'd never been before. Not even when she forgot her entire speech on oral hygiene. She supposed this was the price a person paid for exploding a new galaxy.

"Okay, what is going on?" Gabby finally demanded as she shoved her pillow into the back of the Caprice. "Did I miss something? Did you draw on my face again?"

"No!" Juni and Mason both shrieked at the very same time.

Juni hadn't thought about Gabby's reaction, and had a moment of pure terror when she realized this might change everything. The way Gabby felt about being with them. The way Juni and Mason were with each other. Would he want to kiss her now every single time they were alone? Would he stop telling her all about his dorky discoveries? Because how could you go on and on for fifteen minutes about bacteria and then expect a person to want to kiss you?

Gabby's eyes widened, almost as wide as the time she saw Bill Nye the Science Guy at Fisherman's Wharf.

"My people! You finally did it!" she yelled, and smashed them into a hug.

Everything would be okay. Different, but okay.

They went inside and ate piles of pancakes, eggs and

bacon, and when they had finished cleaning the dishes, Anya walked Juni to the water, where they watched shallow waves lap against the shore.

"I'm going to stay behind," Anya said.

Juni nodded. Until that morning, Juni thought all she really wanted was for Dad to show up and be himself again, to understand what Juni needed and to help her. Now that he was here, trying, Juni realized she wanted something much different. The opposite, actually.

Juni wanted to do the rest of this on her own. With her friends. She wanted to prove she was brave and strong, if only to herself.

She glanced toward the house. Dad stood behind the deck railing talking to Luca. "Do you think he'll let me go on my own?"

"You might be surprised."

"What did you say to him? I thought for sure he was going to make us go home," Juni said.

"I told him he wasn't the only one suffering, and that we all had to find our own way with this, including you," Anya said. "Then I told him that if he didn't let you have this dog, I was moving out."

Juni laughed. "But it's your house!"

"Pfft. Maybe I would have kicked him out, then. He could go live in a tree."

Anya put her arm around Juni's shoulders, and they watched as powerboats whizzed around in the distance, the soft buzz of their engines sounding like flying insects.

Dad appeared beside them. "What are you two conspiring about?"

"I'm going to let you two talk this through." Anya kissed Juni's cheek and walked down the sandy beach, the lake's small waves erasing her footprints as she went.

Juni took a deep breath. "I want to do this by myself, Dad. I want to be able to finish what I started on my own. Well, on our own. With my friends."

He nudged a small rock with his toe. "You do, huh?"

"I'm not mad or anything," Juni said. Even though as she said it, she realized it wasn't true. She was mad. For having to watch her dad disappear into the woods, her mom burrow under the covers every day. To watch the life she'd known turn into one she didn't.

"I let you down," Dad said.

Juni didn't say anything. Because of course he had. They both stared at the lake, the mountains, the puffy clouds inching along on the breeze high above.

"You didn't let me down. You left me alone," Juni finally said.

Dad closed his eyes.

Juni took her dad's arm and leaned into him. They were quiet for a time.

"We'll wait for you," Dad said. "Right here."

The whole time Connor had been missing, Juni had wanted her dad to show up. Now, by staying behind, that was exactly what he was doing.

Life was so strange.

THE WATCH

IT WAS A THREE-HOUR trip from South Lake Tahoe, and Luca drove past the WELCOME TO MAMMOTH LAKES, POP. 8,132 sign at just past noon.

"They named it Mammoth for an overconfident mining company in 1878, not the mammal," Mason said. "They added the word *Lakes* because there are about a hundred lakes around here, all scooped out by glaciers. The company really thought they'd bring in tons of gold and silver, but they didn't."

Mason leaned his head against the window. Gabby picked at her cuticles. Juni had asked Luca to stop playing music, preferring the silence. Anya didn't listen to music in the car, was always saying her mind was busy enough and didn't need a soundtrack. Juni knew just what she meant.

Instead, Juni listened to the natural sounds around her—wind blowing through the half-open windows, tires whooshing against the hot asphalt road. After a while, Juni closed her eyes and swore she could hear when the car went from sunshine into the shade of the trees. She could hear the wide bends in the road, the painted lines under the tires.

When she was tired of listening, she looked at Captain Wilder's Facebook posts again. Pictures of his kids. Elsie with his kids. Elsie playing fetch at one of the hundred lakes nearby.

Preparing herself.

She wrapped her hand around the antler bone necklace, thinking of her tasks. They'd completed the magic spell. Soon, Elsie would be returned to her rightful owner. The only task left was the sacrifice. Juni still had no idea what that might be, but believed she'd know it when the time was right.

The houses grew farther and farther apart until, eventually, Luca turned into a long driveway, a two-story house with redwood siding at the end of it. The house had a big grassy yard in front and an American flag hanging perfectly still beside the front door. It was another hot, dry mountain day.

From the looks of it, every Wilder was in the front yard playing with Elsie.

Elsie. There she was, golden and magnificent. Chasing after a red ball and bringing it back to an older man with white hair. Juni recognized him from Captain Wilder's pictures as Mrs. Wilder's father.

When they parked the Caprice, Elsie stopped her frolicking and sat at the heels of the older man. She was very still, like the flag.

"You ready for this?" Luca said. He turned off the engine.

"Ready," Juni said.

They got out of the car, Mason and Gabby each taking one of Juni's hands. Juni stood tall and pushed her shoulders back. They walked forward as the whole of the Wilder family watched. The smallest Wilder girl held on to her mom. She had a halo of blond ringlets lit by the sun.

"Glad you're here," Captain Wilder said. He was shorter than Juni had imagined, with wide shoulders and muscled arms, a tattoo of a single red rose on his right shoulder.

Elsie stood, alert, and then turned around in a circle, tail wagging. She barked and sat again. She looked at the older man, whining. He finally said, "Go on, girl. Easy, though."

Elsie took off at a run. Straight for Juni.

Juni kneeled down as Elsie reached her, almost knocking her over. She wagged her long golden tail and made little whiny barking sounds, as though she were Juni's long-lost friend and they'd finally been reunited after a snowstorm and a trip through the desert and a journey into outer space and back.

At first, Juni didn't understand. She wasn't much of a dog person, preferring Anya's cats. Dogs didn't particularly like her, either.

Then Juni understood as Elsie nuzzled against Connor's watch.

The watch was Elsie's long-lost friend. Maybe she smelled Connor in the fabric band. Who could ever know?

No one moved or talked, and Juni took her time petting her long golden hair, and whispering into Elsie's ears, *You're a good girl. You did a good job.* Mason took pictures of the two of them with Connor's phone, Captain Wilder with his own. Afterward, introductions were made, including instructions to call Mrs. Wilder's dad Pops.

They all walked to a large deck overlooking a creek and were offered a big pile of finger sandwiches on a green plastic platter. There was a bowl of potato chips and a bowl of fruit, but Juni wasn't hungry.

The youngest Wilder girl, Gertie, cried softly, trying to hide it. She was eight or nine years old. Juni wondered if she knew about Connor, that Juni was Connor's sister, and it was all too much for her.

"So," Pops said as he poured lemonade into small plastic cups. "Why don't you tell us a little bit about Lake Almanor. I've wanted to go there since I was a young man, but never found myself that far north."

Juni found she couldn't talk about small things.

"Thanks for this nice lunch, but we didn't come all this way just to visit," she said.

"Have you had a change of heart?" Captain Wilder said.

"I always wanted to bring Elsie home. I've been bothering my parents since we found out . . . about Connor. It's what Connor wanted for Elsie, too."

Gertie pushed away from the table and went inside. The oldest girl, Jessica, went after her. The middle girl, the one who was exactly Juni's age, Jocelyn, sat staring into her lap.

That's when Juni realized they weren't just upset about Connor. They were upset because they thought Juni had come to take their dog away.

Juni swallowed over the lump growing in her throat.

The Wilders loved Elsie, and Elsie loved them back. Juni was a stranger to her, and even though she knew Elsie would come to love her, because of course she would, now that Juni was here, it didn't feel like the right thing to do anymore.

And then it hit her.

This was meant to be her sacrifice.

Juni was suddenly overcome with the need to leave. She didn't know why she'd come at all, actually, what she'd been thinking. It felt like a plan made by another girl a long time ago. A girl living in a fairy tale once upon a time.

She pushed her chair away from the table, almost knocking it over, and turned to Luca. "Just take me home."

BEFORE THEY LOADED into the Caprice for the trip back to Alice's house, Pops took Juni aside.

"You are extraordinarily brave," he said. His eyes were a blue-gray color, like old jeans.

"I'm a cat person," Juni said, and smiled. She didn't want them feeling any worse than they probably already did.

Pops smiled back. "Give them a little time to get used to the idea. Maybe we can share Elsie. We can have a dog-custody agreement."

"We live six hours away."

"I for one would be happy to drive to Lake Almanor. You can take me fishing."

"That's really nice of you," Juni said.

"It's what we do for family. Elsie is family, and now, by extension, so are you."

Juni felt a numbness creeping over her. She'd come

all this way only to leave Elsie behind. She glanced around, for a buck, maybe, to show himself to her again. She clung tightly to the antler bone so she might feel Connor's radio signal. She wildly hoped the quest itself, even if she didn't bring home the prize, might be enough to break the curse.

But maybe Juni had been fooling herself from the start.

We are only as cursed as we believe ourselves to be.

"I've got to go," Juni said, her chest getting tight.

Pops took her hands in his and gave a firm squeeze. "It isn't over," he said.

But it was for Juni.

NOTIFICATIONS

AFTER A COUPLE of hours in the car, with the only sound being the tires rolling over the asphalt road, Luca's phone gave out another *bing!*

"Look. Captain Wilder posted our pictures," Gabby said.

She handed the phone to Juni. There was a good one of Elsie nuzzling Connor's watch. Juni was smiling in those pictures, her arms wide.

Who even was that girl?

Captain Wilder had written a caption with the pictures: "One big family. Prayers for the fallen soldier our Elsie had to leave behind."

Prayers for the fallen soldier . . .

The fallen soldier.

Connor.

A sob caught in Juni's throat, and the bees swarmed her lungs all at once. "Pull over!"

"What?" Luca said, startled.

"Pull over!"

Luca slowed, but Juni was already reaching for the handle before the car came to a full stop.

She pushed her way out of the car, lungs starting to close. She took a puff from her inhaler and bent over at the waist, resting her hands on her knees.

Think about the bee smoker, Juni. The way it quiets the bees.

Quiet and still.

Quiet and still.

"*Juni.*" A whisper close to her ear.

"What?" Juni said, turning to look at Mason, whose eyes were round and scared. She took another pump of her inhaler.

"I didn't say anything," Mason said.

Juni wondered if it was the trees calling her name. Calling her in.

She caught a flash of white in her peripheral vision. She looked toward the tree line and the dimness of the woods beyond. There it was again, another flash of white, and this time, the galloping sound of hooves.

Juni took off after what she thought might be the white tail of a buck, fighting for breath as she went.

"Juni!" Mason yelled. Luca and Gabby yelled, too.

Ten yards into the woods, twenty. Juni ran and ran after the fading sound of hoofbeats until the only sounds left were her own pounding feet and the swish of leaves and dried needles scattering across the forest floor.

The forest. She'd run smack into the forest. Juni stopped in a small clearing. It was dead quiet. The buck, if it had ever been there, was gone.

Her breath was mostly gone, too.

Juni's legs went weak, so she plopped right down into the red dirt and leaned against a rough-barked tree, her vision narrowing. She'd chased that buck as though she were chasing Connor himself. Or magic. Or the last bits of believing her brother could still come back to her.

She closed her eyes and let herself float to whatever memory dream was waiting.

It was the day Connor had gone missing. An army man had shown up at Juni's door with Father Thomas from Our Lady of Snows, even though Grandpa Charlie had been the only Catholic in the family. And Luca, of all people. Mom's legs had given out right there on the tile entryway floor, and Dad helped her into a chair in the living room, where she began to shake all over. Anya sat at Mom's feet, holding her hand. Juni had ducked in under Dad's arm, attached herself like a barnacle, moved when he moved.

After clearing his very dry throat, the army man

told Juni's family that he was sorry to inform them that Connor Creedy had been reported as missing in action in Kunar province, in Afghanistan, at eleven hundred hours that very day, July 6, after the inspection of a building in the outskirts of a small village. Connor had been in an explosion. There had been an ambush, and a lot of confusion.

"How can he be missing?" Dad had asked.

The army man's eyes flicked to Juni and back to Dad. "We don't have the body yet, sir," he said. "Until we do, we can't, officially, declare him . . . deceased."

"If there's no body, how do you know he's dead?" Juni demanded.

"We have . . . eyewitnesses."

Juni was excused and not allowed back downstairs. She had paced her room, shouting at the mural she'd painted with Connor, the buck in particular, "You promised! You promised you'd come back!" until Luca knocked softly and let himself in.

"Why don't they have his body?" Juni shouted.

Luca leaned against the wall and slid to the floor, his impossibly long legs bent up on either side. Grasshopper legs. "The structure Connor went into was destroyed. Nothing was left. His battalion was ambushed at the same time, so they had to escape before they recovered Connor's body. They'll go back as soon as they can."

"But Elsie survived."

Luca opened his eyes. "Yes. She was blown clear of the building."

"So Connor could have been, too."

Luca and Juni stared at each other. Juni told herself that just because Luca believed Connor was dead—or her parents, or the stupid army man—that didn't make it true.

"Where did he go, then, Juni?" Luca said.

Juni thought for a minute.

"Maybe the bad guys took him. Like they did that guy I heard about on the news. Bergum."

"Bergdahl."

"Right. Maybe he was thrown from the explosion, and someone took him and now they're trying to turn him against his country, like they did with Bergdahl."

Luca stared at the whitewashed planks of Juni's ceiling.

"I'd know it if Connor was dead. He's not dead," Juni finished.

Luca stood. He put his hand on Juni's mural, beside the deer. "He was the only one."

"Who was the only one?"

"Bergdahl. He's the only known POW in Afghanistan. They don't take prisoners over there, Juni."

Juni told him to leave, to stop telling lies, so he did.

JUNI CAME BACK to herself. The bees had calmed. She didn't know how long she'd dreamed. Could have been a minute or an hour or infinity.

Voices called from different directions. Faint. Far away. "Juni!"

A twig snapped in the bushes off to the left, not far from where she sat. She wanted to see the buck so she would know, once and for all, that there might still be something to hope for. She clung tightly to the antler bone, willing it to bring her one last miracle.

"If you're there, please, I need to see you."

There was only silence.

Juni stood, on less wobbly legs, and began walking toward the worried voices of her friends. There wasn't anything left to do. She eventually found Luca on a wooded path near the road.

"What in the . . . ?" Luca ran both hands through his short hair, sending it straight out from his head like he'd been electrocuted. The sudden, unexpected image combined with her light-headedness made Juni snort.

"You think this is funny?" Luca said. "There are black bears in those woods, and cougars and rattlesnakes and ticks! There are no paths! You could have gotten lost! Forever!"

"Or attacked by ticks, I guess," Juni said. Cars flashed through the trees on the road beyond. The tinny sound of music played.

"You think Lyme disease is funny, too?" Luca said. He threw his hands toward the sky and stormed off toward the car. Juni had seen Mr. Tavares make that same gesture a thousand times when the San Francisco 49ers made a stupid play on the field.

Luca turned around once they reached the shoulder of the highway and called for Gabby and Mason. They eventually came out of the woods. Gabby plucked a leaf from Juni's hair.

"What were you thinking?" Luca demanded.

"I saw a deer" was all Juni could say.

"Oh. Well, if you saw a deer, then of course you should run off and chase it! It might be Connor, right?"

A bolt of lightning shot through Juni. Everyone went still.

The Caprice doors were open. Elvis sang, *Are you lonesome tonight?*

"I'm sorry. I shouldn't have said that," Luca said. He stared at the sky before looking at Juni. "Your coloring is awful."

Before she could answer, he went to the station wagon and took out Juni's asthma bag with the peak flow meter.

"I'm fine," Juni said, tired. "I just need to sit here for a minute."

But Luca wasn't having it. He made her breathe into the tube.

"You're at two hundred and ten, Juni. Anya made me promise to call if you hit the low end."

"The low end is two hundred. Besides, what are we going to do? We're almost back to Alice's."

Luca didn't like that. Juni could tell from his frowny eyebrows.

"Fine," he said.

They climbed into the car. When Mason reached for the seat belt, his arm touched Juni's. It was warm and wet-paint tacky from sweat. He wouldn't, or couldn't, look at her.

Juni felt herself shutting off little by little. Like Anya going through the house before bed, flipping one light switch and then the next until everything went dark.

Luca turned the key in the ignition. The engine started, but he didn't move, just looked straight through the window. Thirty seconds passed. A minute. The engine rumbled. He raised his hands to his face. His chest heaved.

Juni had never once in her life seen Luca cry. Not even on the day he'd come to tell them what had happened to Connor.

Luca reached his hand back over the seats, and this time, Juni took it. Gabby grabbed on, too. Then Mason.

So, with all their fingers, hands and arms intertwined, Juni closed her eyes, ready to face the truth she supposed she'd known all along but hadn't been able to believe.

"He's really gone, isn't he?" Juni said, struggling to understand how after almost six weeks, a single post by a perfect stranger on social media had been the thing to break through her belief that Connor might still be okay.

Luca cried quietly, holding tight to Juni's hand. It was the only answer she needed. There was no way Luca would believe Connor was dead if there was any possible way he wasn't.

Connor was gone. Just like everyone had been trying to tell her.

BEE TAMING

WHEN JUNI WAS ten years old, after a particularly bad asthma attack, where she'd thrashed and gagged in a panic for what felt like forever, Connor had asked her to describe what it felt like. That was the first time she'd talked about how her lungs felt like a hive of busy bees.

Most of the time, she'd explained, the bees were quiet, doing their bee business, but then, out of nowhere, they'd swarm and sting, and when that happened, Juni would think, *Maybe this time, I'll die.* She was matter-of-fact when she explained this to Connor. She didn't want him to see how scared she really was.

Connor was brave, so Juni wanted to be brave, too.

The next day, when she was feeling better, Connor drove her to the Bierwagen ranch. They kept fruit trees, peaches and apples, and had a summer stand with all sorts of other fruits and vegetables, like sweet corn and strawberries. Mrs. Bierwagen baked blue-ribbon apple pies and canned the best strawberry jam Juni had ever eaten.

They also kept bees.

When they got to the ranch, Connor spoke to Mr. Bierwagen for a little while before coming back to the station wagon for Juni.

"What are we doing here?" she'd asked, still feeling a little out of sorts from the day before.

"I wanted to show you the bees," Connor said.

"Why?"

He shrugged. "Instinct, I guess."

"Does Mom know about this?"

"No way. And don't you tell her."

Connor dressed himself, and helped Juni, into one of the Bierwagens' beekeeper suits and a long pair of gloves, which made them both look like astronauts. He carefully tucked her suit pants into Mrs. Bierwagen's tall boots, three sizes too big. Juni remembered it had been warm, and the air smelled like tree sap.

Juni walked beside Connor toward the boxlike hives in the middle of the peach orchard. The lanky Mr. Bierwagen was already suited and moving in slow motion around the hives, talking to himself. Then Juni realized that he wasn't talking to himself, he was talking to the bees.

"Virginia is taking an antibiotic for her ear infection, but of course, I brought her some of your honey and it cleared right up. Everyone else is fine and I won't bore you with the details of my arthritis today . . ." He continued in the same soothing voice, "Hello, kids. Move slowly as you approach the hives, and come to the side, not the front."

Juni stopped, ten feet from the hives, and a bee smacked into her face shield. Then another. She was beginning to wonder if Connor had lost his mind. She was shaky, and still feeling as though her lungs weren't completely working like lungs yet, and here he was taking her to a field of bees. All she could think about was their stingers. What might happen if they turned angry all at once.

"Move slow, and they won't head-butt you as much. Those are the guard bees. They're being protective," Mr. Bierwagen said.

Connor started to walk in extra-slow motion, making a static sound into his hand. "One small step for man, one giant leap for mankind."

"Don't make me laugh. They probably don't like that," Juni said.

"You've got to talk soft. Tell them a story," Mr. Bierwagen said. "Like a neighborly visit."

"Once upon a time," Juni started, "there was a girl in a peach orchard and she wanted very much not to get stung by bees."

"There you go," Mr. Bierwagen said. "Just like that."

Juni trembled, scared. But she also felt like she could fly herself, right alongside those bees. She'd never been this close without wanting to run around screaming or batting them away. It was a powerful feeling, to walk among the bees.

"They give their honey, but we don't take all of it. Just enough for ourselves now and then. They pollinate our trees and everyone is happy," Mr. Bierwagen said.

"What if they get mad?" Juni said. "What if they swarm? Bees can kill a person. I read about that in *National Geographic*."

"That's a bit extreme. You're more likely to be struck by lightning than die from a bee sting. Bee swarms are incredibly rare. Especially honeybees."

"How do you keep them calm?" Juni said.

"By staying calm ourselves. That and we try not to interfere with their business. We leave them alone as much as we can, and this."

Mr. Bierwagen lit a small pile of pine needles in a

small metal contraption he was holding and spread the smoke over the top of one of the hives. He slowly lifted the lid about halfway.

"See those slats of wood? Those are called frames. That's where the bees build their honeycomb."

Mr. Bierwagen smoked between the frames and, eventually, took the lid all the way off so they were able to look right inside the workings of the hive. "This is a bee smoker. The smoke makes it so the guard bees' alarm systems are temporarily out of order. It keeps them from giving the signal that something is wrong."

"That's what my inhaler does, sort of," Juni said to Connor. "It calms the bees."

Mr. Bierwagen added a few more pine needles and then handed her the bee smoker. "Give it a whirl."

Juni pulled the little handle and spread the smoke over the hive again. She watched the bees slow, heard their hum soften. They stopped buzzing together on the surface of the hive, and each little bee climbed deep inside the individual honeycombs, hibernating for the moment. She felt herself calm alongside them.

After they were finished smoking, Mr. Bierwagen showed them how to check the frames in the hive for pests, mites or parasites that made the bees sick. They also looked at the bee eggs, little black dots inside each honeycomb, before they put the whole thing back together. Mr. Bierwagen told Juni she was a natural, and gave her a pint of raw honey to take with her.

"Come on over anytime. I could tell they liked you," he said. Mr. Bierwagen stood in the shade of his porch and waved as they drove down the driveway in the Caprice.

On the way home, Connor took Juni to the hardware store and found her a bee smoker. "There are some things you can't control, Juni. Like whether you have asthma. But some things, you can. Like what to think about while it's happening."

Juni didn't think about anything in particular when she couldn't breathe. She just closed her eyes and panicked. Most people weren't helpful, either. A chaperone on a field trip had once shouted at her to "Just breathe!" as though that wasn't the very problem. Panic could make a person lose their marbles.

"Think about how the bee smoker calms the bees, quiet and still. Focus on calm and see what happens. You've got this."

Juni wondered if that might help. And although she was always afraid of when her lungs would betray her next, felt the fear at the back of her mind like a cool shadow, she was a little less afraid that day, the bee smoker gripped tightly in both hands, her brother by her side.

Juni reached for Mason's pinkie. Their kiss felt so far away.

Numb, she watched out the window, green trees and gold grass and blue sky blurring together, and thought about how she had prepared for that kiss. She'd kissed the mirror to make sure her face wasn't doing anything weird. How much lip puckering was the right amount of lip puckering? Too much and it looked like she was whistling, too little and she looked like Gabby when she slept on her back and drooled. Juni wondered if they'd both lean to the same side and crash noses. She wondered what would happen if she had a cold and couldn't breathe through her nostrils. How long was a kiss supposed to last? Should she dry her lips first? Close her eyes?

She had prepared for her quest, too, studying fairy tales in order to gather the right tasks. Stopping for a witch's spell on her way to get Elsie. The sacrifice she had to make. All without her parents' permission or understanding.

Juni prepared herself for asthma attacks. She prepared for speeches, and difficult tests, and snowstorms. Juni prepared for saying goodbye to Anya's foster cats, and Grandpa Charlie when he'd been sick with cancer. And when they found out about Connor going missing, she should have been preparing then, too. For the worst. She didn't know exactly how a person was supposed to do that, but she should have tried.

When they arrived at Alice's, Juni couldn't believe they still had a three-hour drive back home before she could burrow deep into her closet and possibly never come out. She had called ahead and told Dad she had decided not to take Elsie, and could he and Anya please get everything ready so they could drive straight home?

When they arrived at Alice's, Dad and Anya were standing by the lakeshore. They both opened their arms to Juni, who settled into a three-person hug. There, with the clear water lapping at their feet, all three generations rocked and rocked through the sun setting, the seasons passing, the world coming to an end.

A LITTLE BIT LIKE A MIRACLE

TWO WEEKS LATER, Penelope came back.

Living with the family in Quincy and having her name changed to Yolanda was not to Penelope's liking, and she had let it be known. Juni wondered how many scratches those poor boys endured before they realized she didn't belong to them.

Anya was very forgiving when this happened. She appreciated the families who learned they weren't cat people, or realized the cat they'd chosen wasn't the right one, and instead of turning them over to a shelter where they might be put down, they brought them back to Anya. The house was big, and there were many arms to hold them until those kitties found the right place to be.

Apparently, the right place for Penelope was in Juni's room, every day, smack in the middle of her fluffy blue comforter.

Eventually, Juni decided to ask for a family meeting, which they hadn't had since Connor had . . . died.

Died. She'd acknowledged the word, finally, if only in her mind.

She checked herself. Took a few deep breaths. The bees were quiet.

Juni understood now why Anya had given her the journal. It was simple, really. Anya had talked with Juni about it just after they'd gotten home.

"Sometimes, you have to tell yourself a story until you can tell yourself the truth," Anya had said. "Storytelling runs in our family. Maybe this is the true curse."

Anya had smiled when she'd said it, but Juni thought that was truer than true.

"You are a girl with asthma. I am an orphan. But we are so much more than our struggles."

Anya made a big pot of chicken paprikash, her favorite of Abigail's handwritten recipes, and when they gathered for dinner, Juni had a list of requests.

"I want to have a funeral," she said.

Mom closed her eyes. Dad didn't. Anya nodded for Juni to go on.

"You can't lose yourself in the woods all the time, Dad. And, Mom, you can't stay in your room watching dumb TV shows." Juni was firm. "It scares me."

After a few moments, Mom said, "There's nothing to bury, Juni. They still haven't been able to get to where Connor—"

"It doesn't matter," Anya said. "We need to give ourselves something."

Juni wanted this part to be over so they could move on to the next part, whatever that was.

THEY PLANNED A funeral and chose personal items to bury. A kaleidoscope Connor had once told Juni could find gold at the bottom of rainbows. The lug wrench from his toolbox. A little boy's shirt, from all those years ago, the one Connor had wrapped a newborn Juni in before running for her life.

They'd decided to bury Connor's things on the far end of their property; out past the goat pen, through a small wood and into a meadow, a beautiful meadow—with mustard greens and wild grass—that let out onto the lake. It had been Connor's spot. There were two identical cedars with thick trunks sitting ten feet apart, so he'd strung a hammock. It was shaded most of the time, but in the early evening, there was a brief flood of sunlight.

Mrs. Wheeler carved a fine headstone.

CONNOR THOMAS CREEDY

Son

Brother

Grandson

Friend

Hero

At least a hundred people were there. There were Pacific Crest Trail thru-hikers from years past who had stayed in touch with Connor. They all brought heart-shaped stones. There were Sports Nut employees and a few of his junior-college professors. Everyone knew Connor. He'd saved animals and lifeguarded at the lake and volunteered at the fire department, and Juni was certain she would never know anyone like him again.

Overwhelmed by all the people standing in groups, talking and smiling and laughing as they told their own stories, Juni sat in a rented folding chair in the front row and looked into the woods beyond, thinking about the buck she'd seen in the pet cemetery, the one who'd started everything. She wondered where he was out there, if he had a family. If he was all alone.

Mason sat beside her, then Gabby. Juni knew she could do anything now, face anything, all by herself. But she was so glad she didn't have to.

As people began to sit, Juni heard an excited barking coming from the tree line back toward the house. She turned to see Elsie. The Wilders had come to pay their respects, too.

Juni ran all the way across the meadow, happy to greet her, and Elsie was just as happy to see Juni. Or Connor's watch. Juni didn't know, but she didn't care, either. They snuggled and hugged and turned in circles together.

Then a small golden retriever puppy came bounding into Juni and pounced on Elsie's paws. She had the same long hair as Elsie.

Juni looked up to see the Wilder girls, all smiles.

"We got a puppy!" Gertie, the youngest Wilder, declared. "Her name is Roxy."

Juni wrapped her arms around Roxy, who couldn't stop wiggling. She licked Juni's face all over.

"She's yours now," Pops said, and at first, Juni thought he meant Roxy. But then he leaned over and gave Elsie a scratch behind the ears. "Then again, she always was, wasn't she?"

Juni nodded. She took Elsie by the scruff behind both ears and touched their foreheads together. "We've got this now, don't we, girl?"

TRUER THAN TRUE

IT WAS LATE afternoon, the mid-October sunlight fading beneath the tree line. Juni was sitting at the kitchen table working a math problem—Elsie at her feet and Penelope at her elbow—when she heard a car roll down their gravel driveway.

Juni looked out the living room window and saw the same navy-blue sedan that had come all those months ago to tell them about Connor. She almost fell to her knees.

But she didn't.

Instead, she opened the front door to the same army man who had come before. "I'll get my parents," she said before he could speak. Father Thomas had come with him again. Luca hadn't.

Juni walked to the back of the house, where Mom was reading on the porch, an inexplicable feeling of calm spreading through her. It was happening. Whatever slivers of doubt she'd still managed to carry were going to be removed. For better or worse, her family was about to learn the truth once and for all.

Mom must have seen something in Juni's face, because she jumped up, dropping her book on the deck—*bang!*—which made Dad look their way from his place in the goat pen. He came running.

Hearing the car, maybe, Anya had come downstairs, and met them in the foyer. The army man shook each of their hands in turn, and they all went to sit in the living room. For a brief moment, Juni didn't want to know. The not-knowing was torture, but it left a place for hope.

"They have him," the man said with great sorrow. "They found Connor."

SINCE ELSIE HAD come to them, for reasons no one understood, she had gone to Connor's spot in the meadow every day at two o'clock on the dot. And every day, on her way home from the bus stop, Juni walked down the path through the woods to bring her home.

Juni had made a bed for Elsie in her room, had laid one of Connor's favorite sweaters on top. Juni couldn't smell Connor in the fabric anymore, a soapy scent that trailed him after a shower, but Elsie seemed comforted.

She dug her nose under one of the sleeves every night and lay that way until morning, Penelope burrowed into her furry belly.

Juni had taken all the antler drawings off the kitchen wall and moved them to her room, taping them around Connor's mural. She'd taken the antler branches she'd found in the old gnarled tree near Lena's house and mounted them on a rough-cut piece of cedar. Then she'd woven her twinkle lights all around. Her very own gallery.

Through the winter months, Juni had been helping Luca plan his hike on the Pacific Crest Trail coming up in the spring. He was leaving from Campo on April 17 and figured he would reach Chester sometime in late June, early July. Juni, Mason and Gabby were planning to meet him at Domingo Springs Campground with tamales, just like they did every summer.

Juni's family had a small urn with Connor's ashes, and Luca was going to take him along.

One Tuesday in April, just before Luca was set to leave, Juni walked to the meadow from the school bus and Elsie wasn't there, so she stayed and talked to Connor for a while, alone. About her day. About the fact that she liked kissing, but not all the time. About Anya, Mom and Dad. She talked about how they were going to help with Luca's supplies while he walked the PCT, how happy she was that Connor finally got to go, too.

Juni felt him before she saw him.

The buck, standing beside a thick cedar off in the distance. She counted his ten tines.

She stood slowly and, just as slowly, began walking toward him, expecting him to bound away. He didn't.

Juni got within a few feet before he finally took a step back. A tender step. They contemplated each other. She wrapped her hand around her own antler bone, warm from resting against her skin.

There it was again. The shimmering feeling of Connor.

The buck lowered his many-pointed antlers, nosed the ground and then stood tall. It was a full minute, an hour, infinity maybe, before he turned and disappeared into the shade of the thick wood.

Juni felt herself let him go.

"I'll be okay," she whispered.

This was the story Juni chose to tell herself, and she would make sure this one was truer than true.

ACKNOWLEDGMENTS

THERE IS POWER in the stories we choose to remember, the ones we think define who we are. I kept coming back to this idea as I wrote about Juni and her family. At first, all I had was a bunch of loosely connected fragments that didn't make a lot of sense as a story. These are the people who helped me wrangle all those ideas and fragments into a collective whole.

They are generally the same people who help me wrangle myself into a collective whole.

To my writers' group (we really should think of a name for ourselves after seventeen years). Thank you for my books. I could not have done this without the love and support from each of you. Anne Reinhard, Georgia Bragg, Leslie Margolis, Edith Cohn, Victoria Beck, Christine Bernardi, Elizabeth Passarelli and Laurie Young.

Thank you to the Village Cafe crew; Karol Ruth Silverstein, Greg Pincus, Ann Whitford Paul, Dana Middleton, Armineh Manookian, Lissa Price, Lisze Bechtold, Marianne Wallace, Mary Malhotra, Nicole Maggi, Ronna Mandel, Collen Paeff and Joseph Taylor. I almost gave up on this story, and you were all there to remind me I was a writer and this was a story worth finding.

Kristi and Ed Tavares. Thank you for the stories, Ed. You filled in the gaps for the family I didn't get to grow up with. Can't wait to enjoy a tamalada together where I promise not to insult the Dodgers (maybe).

Stacey Barney and Rosemary Stimola. Thank you for your guidance, wisdom and patience. Emphasis on patience. These books wouldn't be what they are without you.

A huge thank-you to Ileana Soon, who created a magnificent cover. You captured the perfect moment.

Thanks to Captain (and uncle) Howard Ruth Jr. for walking me through Grandpa's days flying a Stearman and the official circumstances around a fallen soldier. Any errors in the telling are mine.

Thank you, Dad, for giving me the woods and Lake Almanor.

And thank you to my growing family. Mom, Kevin, Kate, James, Sara, Henry, Elliot and Calvin. I wouldn't have anything to write about without all of you.